PRESIDENTIAL
AFFAIR

THE PRESS SECRETARY'S PASSION

JENNIFER REBECCA

THE PRESS SECRETARY'S PASSION

The moan heard around the world—that's what they're calling me. I'm the toughest Press Secretary there's ever been, and now a sex tape I didn't even know I made is circling the internet. Every day, I face a roomful of the Associate Press, and they ask me to name the man in the video, but I won't. That's not how I play. But will he rescue me from a political nightmare when I need him?

Sometimes, a knight doesn't show up in shining armor. He's videotaped wearing nothing at all.

For all the girls who have ever been told that they're not enough.

You ARE.

PORN STAR PRESS SECRETARY: VIDEO GOES VIRAL!

PROLOGUE

Plot Twist

"**O**hhh... *yes. Yes!*"

I watch as a strong, masculine hand thrusts two fingers into my pussy. My hips arch up to meet him. Swirling wisps of color tease and twirl around his arm in the form of a tattoo, but from this angle, you can't tell what it is in the video. But I clearly have firsthand knowledge of the soldier's cross tattoo that sits on that tan stretch of skin.

"Please!" I hear myself beg.

"Mmm." He chuckles, low and throaty, because he was enjoying teasing me, keeping me on the edge.

"Please!" I needed him so badly. Truth be told, I still do, and thankfully, he's inclined to oblige me, because he shows up in the middle of the night almost every night.

My cheeks heat, and I try to clench my thighs without anyone noticing, but *he* notices. I see him smirk out the corner of my eye. He knows what he does to me and how well he does it too. I watch the screen as he grips his thick, veiny cock in his fist before rubbing the flushed tip through my wetness and then up to stroke my clit, making me bite my lip to keep from crying out, because my torture only seems to egg him on.

It's weird being both humiliated and turned on in a roomful of your friends and colleagues, but it's also nothing I'm new to. I had a full career as a primetime anchor for Eagle News Network, a national cable news channel based out of New York, before Jake named me his Press Secretary. You don't make it this far without a few scars on your arms and knives in your back. Although, even I have to admit that this one takes the cake.

My parents are going to kill me.

"Ahhh," I moan as he finally notches the very tip of him at my center and slides in all the way. That sound is embarrassing. It's a high, keening sound, kind of like a cat in heat, although I guess that's what I was.

"Kill me now," I mumble under my breath.

I remember the moment so well, not only because he showed me a repeat performance last night, but because it was that memorable. He had my body strung so tight and pushed me higher and higher. I was like a lit fuse on a bomb.

The muscles in his thighs and ass flex and ripple

as he pulls out to the tip only to thrust back in, making my tits bounce like a porn star. Is that what I am now? A porn star? He grips my hips so tight in his hands I wore marks for days, just like the ones I carry on my skin now under my wool slacks.

I feel my eyes glaze over. I'm lost in the moment, watching as he pumps into me over and over again. I watch as my hands grip the sheets of the hotel bed tight as I arch my back while he fucks me into oblivion.

And then I watch with everyone else as my jaw drops down on a silent scream and my eyes close as I find completion in a mystery man's arms.

Jake clears his throat. "I think we've seen enough," he says uncomfortably, and the staffer holding the iPad in his hands hits Pause.

"The video was released thirty-seven minutes ago," the staffer says helpfully. "And has been viewed twenty-six million times."

There's a knock at the door.

"Come in," Jake says.

"I was looking for Jules," my assistant says as he pokes his head in the room. "The Press Room is ready for you to brief them on HB 2250."

"Great," I reply, not feeling it at all.

"You don't have to go in there, Jules," Jake says gently. "We can send in someone else. Hell, I'll do it myself."

"Normally, I would say no to that," Rick inserts.

"But for you, I'd even do it."

"Come on, guys." I laugh, but it lands flat, even to my own ears. "This happens every day. I'll be old news by tomorrow. Time to get back on the horse."

"Jules, you don't have to be brave in here," Jake tells me. He knows me well for someone who's new to my life. Marrying my bestie, Grace, was the smartest thing he ever did, and he loves her so much he'd do anything for her. Including protect her idiot best friend from a sex tape scandal.

I shrug one shoulder like it's no big deal. "Nah, I can't let them smell my fear. Besides, I'm surprised it hasn't happened before now."

And then I walk out of the Oval Office and down the hall toward the White House Press Room to brief a bunch of great white sharks on a congressional bill the president vehemently opposes and, plot twist, all while my boobs are bouncing around the internet like a porn star and the knowledge that the world has now seen my "O" face.

WHERE IS CHIEF OF STAFF'S DAUGHTER?

CHAPTER 1

Kicking and screaming

One month earlier

The White House

"**M**a'am," his voice rumbles in a southern drawl, and not in a nice way. I'm sure it would be nice if he were nice to me, but for some reason I do not know, Captain Ryan Black cannot stand me. "I need you to come with me."

"What? Why?" I ask. If there's something seriously wrong, I need to know. It's part of my job as the White House Press Secretary to be ahead of any and all situations and present statements to the Press on what is going on and how the President is responding to it. So my question is not at all out of left field.

"That's not for you to know, ma'am," he says curtly, and honestly that's utter bullshit.

"Then no," I respond. "I'm not going with you."

Let him put that in his pipe and smoke it.

"Ma'am," he repeats, and I can see the muscles in his jaw working, so he's clearly trying to hold tight to his patience with me, but there he goes ma'am-ing me again. I get that he's from Texas and they ma'am there and it's a military thing, but the way he says it to me doesn't seem very nice. Now, with Grace and Cara, he's as sweet as can be, but with me, he's all piss and vinegar, and I am over it. "With all due respect, you're coming with me."

I can barely hold back the frustrated sigh that's threatening to burst free. I like to be direct, and I like people who are direct with me, so this talking around me in circles isn't really making me feel all warm and fuzzy on the inside.

"With all due respect," I reply, because I think we've danced around each other enough for one day and I have some two-day-old mu shu chicken in my fridge I either need to eat or toss and I'm really looking forward to eating it. So it's time to get this show on the road. "When someone starts a statement with 'with all due respect,' in my experience, they mean absolutely none will be given."

"That's probably true."

Wait, what? Did he… did he just admit he doesn't respect me? What an asshole.

"You don't respect me?" I ask, carefully holding my facial expression so I give nothing away, even though on the inside I'm steaming mad.

"I see nothing but a spoiled princess, ma'am," he answers, and wow, that really stung. I wonder what I ever did to make him dislike me so much. "So now it's time to get your spoiled ass in the fucking car."

I don't fucking think so. "No."

"This was not a question. It's an order," he growls, and the deep, rumbly sound sends a shiver down my back and tingles in other places.

No! We are not attracted to the rude Neanderthal. He is an asshole. We decided we were done with men in New York.

I had been dating a co-anchor before Jake hired me to run his press room. He was tall, blond, and I suspected he was also Botoxed. I thought everything was going well, and in my head, I even started planning a spring wedding.

But then I had news story after news story pulled from me and handed to a young man fresh out of some state school in California and who had absolutely no business at a National News Channel such as Eagle News. He hadn't paid his dues yet.

And then one evening, I used my key to surprise my boyfriend, only I was the one who got the surprise. They're still together to this day, and the invitation to their fall wedding is pinned to my refrigerator. I wasn't even hurt about it. We didn't love each other.

Before that, it was another cheater, this time with a woman—or I should say a lot of them. And before that, it was a guy who stole my checking account number. So by the time my last boyfriend found his one and only not in me, I was over trying.

And I was not going to let this highhanded alpha male use me as a doormat, whether he had a nice voice and an attractive amount of silver at his temples or not. The way he filled out the trousers of his uniform wasn't going to influence that decision either.

I was done.

"Then you're going to have to drag me kicking and screaming," I said as I landed my hands on my hips in the universal stance of a pissed-off woman.

What I did not realize in all of my introspection was that Captain Black was not a man to be challenged like that. If I realized that, maybe I would have made a polite but quiet excuse before I scurried away in order to regroup so I could fight another day.

No, I got in his face, which was not how I was raised. I'm Julia Fairchild of the New Haven Fairchilds, although we have summer houses in the Hamptons as well as the Keys and Hawaii. I was raised to be a lady, socialite, and then a trophy wife. And in my thirty-three-year tenure in the position, I had done none of those things.

I also apparently didn't learn any real-world lessons. Otherwise, I would have taken a measured step back when I saw his eyes flare as I threw down my gauntlet. I would have seen the smirk that flitted across his lips and maybe also that the crotch of his jeans was a little more fitted than it was ten minutes ago. Or all of the above.

But I didn't, and now I'm going to learn a real-life lesson handed to me by the sexiest man on the planet who also just so happens to be an asshole.

"Be careful what you wish for, princess."

And then before I could utter a single word, but not before I could open my mouth to try, he bends at the middle and comes at me, driving his shoulder into my belly, making me let out a soft "oof." And then I'm going up… up… up as he stands and bounces me on his shoulder to get a better hold on me before he carries me through some of the not so well-known exit tunnels to a dark, unmarked SUV.

He beeps the locks with a key fob and pulls open the back door before tossing me inside. I try to pull at the door handles, but he has the child lock engaged! I let out a little growl as I try the door again.

He pulls open the driver door, climbs behind the wheel before taking one look at me in the throes of my escape attempt, and just says, "No," and then he starts the car like kidnapping is no big deal.

"This is insane," I snap. "Just let me go."

"No," he repeats as he drives. He doesn't even bother to look my way, like I'm not a person; I'm a nuisance. "This is important."

"Well, I would know that if you would tell me what this is," I say snottily like the spoiled brat he proclaimed I am.

Fortunately for me—or unfortunately, as the case may be—he doesn't say anything else to me as he drives me through D.C. and then farther and farther until we pull up to a deserted farmhouse. He pulls the car into a faded red barn next to several others and parks the car.

Captain Black steps down from the vehicle, and I watch as he closes his door and pulls open the rear door on that side, not the one I'm sitting next. I think he's done with his barbarian routine and will finally let me have some answers, because one look at me would show I'm spitting mad. Although, one look at him should have told me the same thing, only I wasn't paying close enough attention. And then he wraps his large hand with its deliciously calloused fingertips around my slim ankle and yanks me out of the car.

"Not this again," I mumble, but again he gives me no reply.

He catches me and throws me over his shoulder once more before storming up the back steps of the home. I don't even bother to scream, because there's no one around for miles and miles.

I manage to wiggle out of his arms with a quick elbow to his not at all soft middle. I cannot believe the nerve of this man! Who does he think he is, hauling me around and manhandling me like this? I storm my way through the house, determined to get away from him, when he reaches for me again, grabbing me by the back of my arm.

"Would you kindly get your paws off me!" I snap

before coming to a halt when I notice the full room. I'm instantly alert. "What's going on here?"

"Sit down, Jules," Jake says quietly. "This is serious."

"What's happened?" I ask before I settle myself on the arm of a sofa.

"Rachel has been taken," Rick says to the room.

Jake closes his eyes for a second before opening them again, and when he does, they burn bright with determination and retribution. This is what I love about our president, not only for our country, but for one of my closest friends. That loyalty is hers to harness, and I am over-the-moon happy she has someone like that.

"Is there any connection between her kidnapping and this morning's revelations?" Jake questions.

"I think so," Rick answers quietly, and my gut clenches.

I don't have any children, and at the rate I'm going, I probably never will, so I can't imagine what they're feeling. But it crushes my heart and lights a fire in my gut. What kind of monster would take a child? I know now that I will do whatever they need me to do to help. I haven't been friends with Cara and Rick for years like I have Grace, but that doesn't matter. These are my people, and for them, I'll go to battle.

I met Grace—and our other bestie, Angie—at NYU during Freshman Rush. I don't know how or why but we stuck. Even though Angie has since moved to Texas and married the love of her life, a former professional football player and is in the middle of living her dream and popping out beautiful football loving babies, Grace and I remain close with her. Grace and I have been inseparable. Although, that's easy to do when you stay in the same town.

About a year ago, Grace was swept off her feet by then hot bachelor U.S. Senator Jake. It was hate at first sight for Grace but good old Jake had some tricks up his sleeve. With the help of his long time friend and campaign manager, Rick, Jake was able to win over Grace.

When Jake won the big election the first thing he did was sign Rick and I on as his inner circle. Rick is now one hell of a Chief of Staff and I make the press room my bitch. I absolutely love my job.

We had thought that what your saw was what you get with the always grouchy Rick but that couldn't have been farther from the truth. Imagine everyone's surprise when his long lost ex-wife showed up with their adorable daughter. Grace and I instantly took them in. They're part of the family now.

"Is this place even secure?" Captain Black bites out. I turn only my head to look at him where he stands against the far wall. He's with the group but separate, and that pings in my heart, but I don't know why.

And he's angry.

His voice stings as it whips around the room, and I realize he's angry at *me*. What the hell could I have done now?

"Yes," Jake says calmly. "This property is secure and off public records. Rick and I meet here often."

"All right." Ryan nods.

"What makes you think the two events are connected?" Jake asks.

I watch with rapt attention as Rick folds Cara into his arms while he sits on the arm of the sofa where she's sitting. The move is intimate and familiar, and I wonder how long this has been going on. It was clear months ago that they knew each other, but I was always under the impression that Rick hated her, and poor Cara just seemed so… *sad*. There's clearly more here than meets the eye.

"Nine years ago, Cara and I were married," Rick says to the room. Grace and Jake's faces are both carefully blank. They obviously knew the big secret.

"What?" The word falls from my lips before I can stop it, and I feel my eyes go wide at this news. Holy shit. I look back, over my shoulder, and my eyes land on Ryan.

"And nine years ago, Cara left me when Jake and I were deployed." Ryan's eyes narrow on Cara for a split second. His judgement is evident, and he's clearly not impressed with the way she treated a brother in arms.

"Ouch," Grace whispers.

"She was blackmailed," Rick adds.

"What?" Jake barks out.

"I was sent pictures of Rick overseas and told that

if I didn't leave him, he would die by friendly fire that night," she answers quietly. Oh shit shit. I'm not sure I wouldn't have done the same thing in that situation to protect someone I loved. My respect for Cara ratchets up more than a few notches.

"So you left," Jake adds.

"Yes."

"To protect Donovan," Ryan adds, and I can see by the way his face softens that he's changed his opinion of her.

"Yes," she confirms his assumptions.

"When was this?" Jake asks.

"March," Rick and Cara reply at the same time.

"About when we were assigned to the cartel op?" Jake asks with a raised brow.

"The one and the same," Rick growls.

"Well," Jake says, steepling his fingers together. "That is interesting."

"That's what I thought," Rick says casually, making Captain Black lose his patience.

"Care to share with the fucking class?" Ryan barks.

"Yes," Jake says with a smile, clearly enjoying riling up his aide. "As you know, Rick and I were on the same SEAL team. On one deployment, we were presented with an off-the-books mission. It seemed… *off*. But we were young and dumb and weren't necessarily in the market to question orders that came from way above our pay grade."

"Or we would have, if I hadn't been on a one-man suicide mission," Rick adds, making Cara let out a pained gasp.

"No," she whispers.

"I was pretty messed up after my wife left me," he says. "I jumped at any mission they gave me. It didn't matter how dangerous. And if it seemed like a one-way ticket, even better."

"Rick—" she starts, but they aren't going to give her the time to fall into her own pit of despair.

"And I was there for my brother," Jakes inserts. "And I had no intention of running for office when my dad retired."

"But this one was different," Rick finishes.

"Different, how?" Ryan asks.

"It didn't go as planned and people died," Rick admits.

"And you think this mission is connected?" he asks Rick and Jake.

"Yes," they both say in unison.

"Why?"

"Because of what the blackmailers mentioned," Jake says.

Blackmailers? What the fuck is going on here? Now Jake is being blackmailed too? Ryan obviously knows what these two are talking about, and I realize I was cut out of the loop. What fucking bullshit. I've been nothing but a team player the entire time, and these macho men cut me out. How can I do my job if they don't give me the tools to do it?

The only thing keeping me from losing my absolute shit right now is the knowledge that I have to keep it together and stay focused so I can do what needs to be done to help find Rachel. Because in all of this mess, she's just a little girl caught up in it all, and none of this is her fault.

"They said 'Old ghosts will rise, and others will pay the price. Pass the bill or pay the price,'" Black recites.

"No," Rick corrects. "It said the 'Old Ghost' as in singular and—"

"My old callsign," Jake finishes.

"Someone knows way more than they should," Rick says, sending chills down my spine.

"Who else would know about that op?" Ryan asks.

"We should call Wes and Lee," Rick adds.

"Just to warn them, but that op was after they got out," Jake agrees with him.

"I'll call him now and put it on speakerphone," Rick suggests, and Jake nods in agreement.

Rick slips his phone out of his pocket and swipes his finger across the glass to unlock it when he types in his code. He selects the phone app and dials in a number by heart before pressing the speakerphone button. The ringing sound fills the room, and we all collectively hold our breath.

"Special Agent O'Connell," a deep voice answers. Grace and I had met the sexy SAIC and his beautiful detective wife back in New York. I like them both immensely.

"It's Donovan," Rick says.

"And Chancey," Jake says.

"Well why wasn't I invited to the party?" Wes laughs.

"It's not so much of a party," Rick says darkly. "But we'll get to that in a minute."

"You wouldn't be near Goodie's office, would you?" Jake asks.

"No," Wes answers. "With Claire on desk duty now that she's as big as a house, and if you repeat that, I will not only deny ever having said it, but I will help her hide your miserable fucking bodies."

"So pregnancy agrees with your blushing bride?" Jake laughs.

"No fucking way," Wes grumbles. "I love her, but she's a monster."

"That sounds like how Angie was." I laugh, thinking of our old college roommate who now lives in East Texas with her husband and adorable daughter.

"I was just thinking the same," Grace agrees with me.

"So Goodie isn't around?" Jake asks, bringing the conversation back around.

"No," Wes says, and I can hear his heavy sigh across

the line. There's clearly a lot going on in New Jersey. "With Claire on desk duty and miserable, he's having to cover her field work. There's something heating up in the area that sounds like it might be ready to shift to my office, but I'm actually out of town at the moment working another case. I'll be happy to pass the word on though."

"Something has come up here, and it looks like it's linked to a mission we carried out after you guys got out, but I just wanted to give you the heads up," Jake says.

"Funny you should mention that," Wes murmurs, not sounding like it's funny at all. "The case I'm working on?"

"Yeah?" Rick says.

"I'm in Virgina. Palmer is dead."

"What?" Rick asks.

"When?" Jake questions.

"It's recent," Wes says. "He ate a bullet."

"Fuck," Rick bites out. "I didn't know he was struggling."

"No one did," Wes replies. "I had just seen him at Claire's shower. He seemed fine."

"I'm sorry," Rick says. "So fucking sorry."

"Me too." Wes sighs. "Anyways, it sounds like there's more to your story than 'some shit came up over an old mission.'"

"You'd be right," Rick says. "Someone kidnapped

my daughter after blackmailing my wife."

"I'll be at your house in D.C. at nine," he says and then disconnects.

"Typical Wes," Rick grumbles, making Jake laugh. "Still calling orders."

"Looks like the gang is getting back together." Jake smiles.

"So what now?" Ryan asks.

"I think we need to figure out who could be behind this," Jake says.

"And we need a plan to get my daughter back," Rick growls.

"Oo-rah," Gus, Joe, and Ryan all shout, startling me a bit. I had forgotten everyone in the room. And Marines are weird.

"I can't help but feel like this all goes back to getting to the president," Ryan says. "I don't know the story as well as you do, but—"

"But what?" Rick asks.

"It all sounds to me like someone is moving the pieces on a chessboard, and it all goes back to the president. I think we need to go way back before they were married. Before Mrs. Donovan was even in the picture."

"We're going to need sustenance for that," I say, clapping my hands together. "Is there any food in this joint?

"The freezer and pantry should be fully stocked,"

Rick replies. "I don't come out here enough to keep perishables in the fridge."

"Excellent," I respond and jump up to move into action. Grace struggles under her very pregnant belly to hop up and follow me, but she doesn't make it.

"Fuck," she bites out. "Jules, give me a hand or I'll never get up."

"Well, why didn't you say something, darling?" Jakes asks with a twinkle in his eyes before he lifts her up like she weighs nothing at all and sets her on her feet. "There you go."

"Yes, thank you," she snaps.

"Cara?" I call her name a few minutes later when I see her wander into the kitchen. She looks lost, and it scares me. "Honey, are you okay?"

"I don't know," she says. "They're kind of scary out there."

"I think with you they're more bark than bite."

"What about with you?" she asks me, making me laugh.

"What about me? I can run with the big boys. I don't need to be cared for."

"I came to help with… whatever it is that's going on in here," she says, making Grace and me laugh a little. "What am I missing?"

"We were gossiping," Grace admits.

"I don't doubt it." Cara sighs. "Why leave me out? That's not fair!"

"We were talking *about* you," she admits.

"Well, thanks for that."

"It was all good," Grace says quickly.

"It was brave what you did," I say softly.

"Or stupid," she admits. "I feel like I've done nothing but play into their hands. Whoever they are."

She walks over to the coffee maker and begins to tinker with it. Grace and I both keep an eye on her as she pauses her actions to grip the counter in her hands and let her head fall forward. We stay quiet while she obviously grapples with her composure and control.

And then she just fucking loses it as she grabs the bag of coffee grounds, hurls them across the kitchen, and screams. It's an eerie fucking sound as she shrieks, and for second, I don't know what to do.

"Jake!" I hear Grace shout as Cara drops to her knees and slams her hands against the floor and all the mess.

"Ryan! Rick!" I yell as I race for the kitchen door. "Come quick!"

Rick scoops her up into his arms and begins to try to soothe her. I send a look around the room, and everyone files out to give them the privacy they need to deal with her emotional collapse, one that we could all see was coming a mile away.

We stand silently around the old-fashioned living room. No one utters a single word. Poor Cara, so lost in her grief. How would I feel if I was a mother and my only child had been taken? Just as awful, no doubt.

I watch out the corner of my eye as Jake leans into Grace, giving her the comfort that they both need right now. He lays his hand over hers on her round belly, and the moment is so intimate I have to look away. I feel so lost, because these are my people, and I would do anything for them. Yet at the same time, it feels like I no longer have a place within the circle. Everyone has moved on.

After a while, Rick walks down the stairs with a haggard look on his face.

"I'm not sure there's much else we can do here tonight," Ryan says from behind me, and I can't help but agree.

"I agree," Jake adds. "I think we head back to D.C. and keep our eyes and ears open. Report to the group if anything changes."

"Agreed," Rick says.

"Agreed," Ryan repeats, and I just nod. The men were more having a meeting of the minds anyway. I'll get my reports to give from Rick and Jake when needed. Otherwise, I just have to mind my Ps and Qs, as they say.

"Let's go," Ryan barks, startling me. It would only be more embarrassing, the way he's ordering me around, if he snapped his fingers at me like I was a dog. His terse command goes a long way to remind me how I got to this delightful little farmhouse earlier this afternoon. Not by choice, but by force.

I narrow my eyes on him, but he doesn't see, because he's already turned away and is walking toward the door. Obviously, he feels like I'm going to follow him like a good little puppy.

"We can give you a ride back to D.C. if you'd like," Grace says softly. I look back over my shoulder to her, and she has a concerned look on her face. I can't let her worry about me too. That can't be good for the baby. Besides, we all already have enough to worry about with Cara, Rick, and Rachel.

"Oh, I'll be fine," I say, smiling my evil, "I'm up to no good" smile. "It's not me you should be worried about."

"Give him hell," she says, and Jake fakes a cough to hide his laughter, but when he looks at me, I see his eyes are dancing. Gus looks to his feet.

"Don't worry, I will."

I hug my friend one last time before looking to the stairs and send up a little prayer that Cara will be all right and that Rachel will be found safe. Then I turn on my heels and follow Ryan's path through the house, back to the kitchen, and out the back door, where he is waiting for me.

"What took you so long?" he snaps, and I look at him. He's angry, and I don't understand why. I'm the one who should be angry, and here he is, still treating me like garbage. I don't get it.

"I was saying goodbye to my friends," I answer, even though I don't really feel like he deserves one.

I'm right when the next words out of his mouth follow.

"Those people in there are not your friends."

"I beg to differ," I say, rolling my eyes. "I've known Grace since college."

"The Grace you knew is gone, and those people are the leaders of this country," he says. "They are not your friends, and if you think for one second that you are not expendable when it comes to the safety of this country, you are *mistaken*."

He pulls the passenger door open for me, and I slide in just before he slams it closed. I do not turn to him as he walks around and climbs in the driver seat. He does not look at me as he turns the key to start the engine or as he backs out of the old barn and heads back to D.C. In fact, he acts as if I'm not even there the entire two-hour drive back to the city and then on through to my home in Virginia. And I'm all too happy to return the favor. I opt to spend the trip with my arms folded across my chest and my eyes trained straight through the front windshield.

When he pulls into my driveway, I can't move fast enough as I grapple with the buckle of my seatbelt and snatch up my purse.

"Stay here," he barks at me, and I see red.

"I don't think so."

"I said stay here," he repeats. "I'll walk you to your door."

"I'm a big girl, Captain," I snark. "I don't need you

to see me to my door."

"Well I'm going to do it anyways, duchess, so get fucking used to it."

I barely hold in a scream as he steps down from his door, stomps around to my side, and yanks open my door before hauling my body down from the SUV. Ryan is such a dick, and I wonder not for the first time when I started thinking of him as Ryan and not Captain Black.

He wraps his large hand around my upper arm and practically perp-marches me to my front door. I don't believe this. Who does he think he is, treating me this way? I've just pulled my keyring out of my brown leather hobo purse when they are snatched out of my hand, and Ryan expertly selects the key to my front door like he does it every day.

I stand there stunned, and I'm sure my mouth is hanging open as he unlocks the deadbolt and pushes the door open. And then, since I was still standing there in stunned silence, he puts a palm to my belly and gently shoves me through the door.

I'm about to tell him to go straight to hell when he follows me over the threshold and kicks the door shut behind him.

"Are you over your fucking snit?" he asks, and I narrow my eyes on him. What a dick!

"Are you done being an asshole?"

"No," he answers. "Not fucking likely."

"Then no, I'm also not over my snit."

I don't know who moves first, and likely, I never will. It could have been me, as I jump in his arms, or it could have been Ryan as his arm struck out to grab me. All I know is I'm in his arms with my legs wrapped around his lean hips as he crushes his mouth down on mine.

I don't hesitate when he opens over me and let him thrust his tongue into my mouth. I dig my fingers through his hair and pull him closer. I can't get enough, and I hold him to me as tight as I can.

Thanks to my skirt, his hard length presses against the gusset of my panties through the worn, soft denim of his jeans, and the feeling sends an electric current through my body. I rock my hips against him, needing more, more, more, and he grips my ass tight in his hands as he groans into my mouth.

Ryan dips his hand down the back of my panties to between my thighs. He circles my opening with a finger, just barely grazing my clit with each pass. I tip my ass back, needing his fingers on me, which takes me away from his cock, but he's so good with his fingers that it doesn't disappoint when he dips just the tip of one inside me on a pass.

"Fuck, fuck, fuck," he bites out. "My prissy duchess is wet for me."

"Yes," I pant as I reach my hips back for more while I slip my arms between us and unbuckle his belt.

"Fucking drenched for me."

I get half the buttons down on his fly before I give up and reach inside. I wrap my hand around his thickness and barely register as he curses I'm so intent on my goal, and I pull his cock free. It's long and hard and thick, and I want it. I pump him in my hand, wanting him to feel as crazed and as far gone as I am.

"Show me your tits," he growls as he hits my clit with a fingertip, distracting me from my mission. "Now."

I nod as I let go of him and slide my hands up between us to undo the buttons on the front of my poplin blouse. My hands shake as I go one by one down to my belly button, and he watches me with dark eyes, burning my skin as I go.

"Show me," he says as he brushes my clit again, and I part the material of my blouse, revealing my lace bra. I pull the cups down, exposing my pink nipples, and I immensely enjoy the flare of his pupils as he takes me in, so I decide to push him a little more by pinching my stiff peaks.

His response is everything.

Ryan roars as he drops forward, taking the tip of my breast into his mouth and sucking hard as we fall. He controls the impact by taking the brunt of it on his knees before my back hits the floor. I can feel the cool tile of the entryway through my blouse, but it doesn't matter, because I am on fire.

He scores my nipple with his teeth as he rips out the seam of my panties before thrusting two fingers deep inside me.

"Yes," I pant.

He lets go of my nipple with a pop, taking his hard cock in his hand and guiding it to my opening before he thrusts deep inside me. I let out a gasp at the intrusion, and he doesn't let me adjust to the thickness of him as he fills me over and over.

His body covers mine completely, and I slide my hands up the back of his T-shirt and score my nails down his skin as he takes me. And he does take, but he also gives, because with each punishing drive, he brings me closer and closer to the orgasm that's barreling down on me.

I pant and grasp and just hold on as he pounds into me over and over, and then like an elastic band that's been stretched too far, I snap. I was wrong about the climax that I knew would be huge. It isn't huge; it destroys me. It wrecks me as it ravages through me, so much so that I'm only able to register Ryan's snarl as he comes.

And then he's silent.

He's so quiet and still as his breathing settles, and I feel something not good fill the room. I should have braced, but I didn't, because I foolishly thought we were having a moment. Ryan and I had come together, and it was more than stolen touches this time. I let it come into my head that maybe he had come to care for me when he had given no indication so. But I find out that I was wrong, so very wrong, when he slaps the tile next to my head with his palm.

And then he pulls out quickly and rolls, pushing up to his feet. He keeps his back to me as he tucks himself back in his jeans and does up the buttons and then his belt. And the whole time, he stays so fucking silent that my heart begins to sink right through my body and down to the cold floor he's left me on.

"Ryan?" I ask, and I hate that my voice sounds soft and unsure, because that is not who I am or who I ever want to be. And furthermore, I do not like that he's made me sound that way. But still, right now, I can't help it. And I am sorrier when he turns around and glares at me.

"You got your piece of my dick, duchess, but you won't get your fancy claws in me," he snarls. "This was it. There won't be a repeat."

"What?" I whisper, horrified. I feel heat hit my face, and I grab at the parted material of my blouse, trying to cover myself belatedly.

"You heard me," he says. "You got one fuck, and now we're done."

"Nice mouth," I snap.

"Manners come with the uniform," he replies, drawing my attention to the jeans I had never seen him in before, the ones that fit him so very well. "But they're not for you."

And with that parting shot, he turns on his heels and slams my front door behind him, leaving me sprawled on the floor of my foyer half dressed, with his cum slipping out of my body.

"I think I made a mistake," I say to myself before I push to stand and feel the sting of muscles that haven't been used in a while. I lock the front door, and then I walk upstairs to my bedroom and undress. I pull on a heavy, oversized sweatshirt that falls to my knees. I don't bother brushing my hair or washing my face. What's the use? There's no sense in tending to the outside when the inside is looking so ugly.

And then I climb under the covers of my big bed all alone and think about each and every choice I've made in my career and in my life that led me to this moment. I feel each one, I own it, and then I let it go before I finally let myself drift off to sleep on my pillow damp with tears, knowing I'm always going to be all alone, and that's okay. I'll make peace with it.

PRESIDENT CHANCELLOR VETOES GLOBAL BILL

CHAPTER 2

Vetoed

"**G**ood morning, everyone," I say to the room when I step up to the podium. "President Chancellor has vetoed House Bill 2250."

The room is silent for a moment, and then it explodes with a cacophony of voices. Every single reporter in the room is shouting questions at me and all at the same time.

This morning when I entered the White House offices, the official notice had gone out throughout my office. The president had decided early this morning that he was going to veto the bill that would take the bulk of the weapons, money, and global power that the United States holds and give it to several nations who harbor hostility toward the U.S.

"While I'm sure you all have many questions, this

is developing now," I explain. "The President has not hidden his concerns over what he considers a dangerous bill that was laid out to the house floor. President Chancellor has expressed these concerns at length and had many productive talks with the members of Congress. And after asking many questions, the president feels that he and the American people have been left with less answers and more questions.

"So at this time, he is exercising his right to veto. Thank you. That will be all for today."

And then I turn and walk out of the room to the tune of questions shouted at my back.

"Holy shit, Jules," Carter, Grace's assistant, says when I clear the doors and am in the staff-only hallway. "That was fucking hot as hell. If I was into girls, I would be totally into you."

I bark out a laugh. Carter is such a good guy. I've known him and his husband for years, because he worked with Grace in New York, and we all swam in the same circles. His comments go a long way to elevate my mood.

"Thanks, Carter." I smile at him.

"Grace sent me," he says. "She said you were having a shit day and wanted to know if you'd like her to watch you drink a bottle of wine before she has someone take you home."

"That's so Grace." I laugh. Just because she's adorably pregnant and can't drink, she doesn't want me to go home alone after a long day. And she doesn't even know the half of what happened with Ryan.

"I know, right?"

"Tell her that I'm fine and am going home to drown my frustration in carbs not booze," I reply. Carter watches me closely, like he's trying to decide the veracity of my statements. "Really. I'm fine."

"Oh all right," he says. "But if she shows up at your house unannounced…."

"She can't," I remind him. "She can't go anywhere without a massive team of secret service agents.

"True." He smirks. "But I'm sure she could find someone to come check on you."

"Don't go there," I say over my shoulder as I continue on down the hall.

I head to my office and grab my bag. I pull my keys out so I'm ready and head through the offices toward the exit. I see Captain Black out the corner of my eye talking to someone, and I just keep moving. He waves to me, but I don't stop. I just keep moving through the building.

When I reach the external door, I push it open and take my first deep breath of the entire day. I'm just to my car when I hear someone shout in the distance, but I ignore it. Instead, I pull open the driver door and toss my bag on the front seat.

"Julia!" I hear, and I look to see Ryan at the exit to the offices. I let out a frustrated breath, plaster a fake smile on my face, and toss Ryan a wave I don't mean before I drop down into my cute little Mercedes. As I pull out of the parking lot, I see him running toward me between the cars.

But that's a worry for another day.

It takes about an hour with D.C. traffic to get to my suburban neighborhood in Virginia. I don't listen to the radio, because I can't let the news updates get to me, so I connect my phone to Bluetooth so I can listen to my playlist. That goes out the window when Ryan calls for the third time, and I dismiss the call for the third time, and I'm tempted to throw my phone out the window. So I hold the button down to shut it off and toss it to the seat next to me.

Rachel is still missing, and while Rick looks like he's keeping it together, I know he's frustrated. I haven't seen Cara since the other day, and I need to check in on her. Maybe tomorrow I'll be able to check up on her.

I pull into my garage, scoop up my phone and keys, and toss them in my bag. I let myself in through the garage, which leads to a small laundry room off the kitchen, kicking off my heels by the door and dropping my purse on the kitchen counter.

I'm starving.

I need to figure out dinner and soon. I open the fridge, and there's some wilted lettuce and a bottle of coffee creamer. That is less than promising. I pull my phone from my purse and power it back up so I can order a pizza. It takes a full minute while it dings with missed calls and a few angry voicemails from Ryan which consist of a tersely spoken "call me" and "I'm done fucking around." And then I dial my favorite pizza place and order a large pepperoni for delivery. It's not New York pizza, but it'll do.

I don't wash my face or change into sweats, because it would be bad form to open the door for the delivery kid looking like a mess and get spotted by paparazzi. It doesn't happen often, but after a day like today, I wouldn't discount the possibility.

So instead, I pad to the bar in my stocking feet and grab a brand-new pinot noir. I pull the cork and pour myself a glass. I guess I was lying after all when I told Carter that my plans excluded booze.

The doorbell rings, and I grab a twenty out of my wallet and another ten to tip.

"Here's your pizza, Ms. Fairchild."

"Thanks," I tell him before taking the piping-hot box and closing the door.

I set it on the coffee table and grab my glass and the bottle. I settle on the couch and eat more pizza than I should and finish the bottle while watching *Murder She Wrote* reruns on cable.

With a heavy sigh when I realize it's grown late, I pick up the pizza leftovers and toss them in the fridge before putting my wine glass in the sink and the bottle in the recycling bin. I make sure the doors are locked and then turn out the lights downstairs before padding quietly up the stairs.

My bedroom is dark when I enter, and I don't turn the lights on. I toss my heels I picked up on my way through the kitchen into the closet and untie the sash belt of my dress before I work the small buttons down the front with my fingers.

"Christ, it's like watching your Christmas present unwrap itself," Ryan says from where I now see he's lounging on my bed with his legs crossed at the ankles and his hands behind his head.

Of course, I do what any single woman from the city does when she realizes there's a man in her bed when she thought she was alone in the house.

I scream bloody murder.

"Shh," he soothes, and he's in front of me before I can even blink.

"What are you doing here?" I ask accusingly when it feels like my heart has slowed to the point that it's still beating like a racehorse but not so fast I'm about to die.

"You didn't answer your phone," he says like that explains everything.

"So you broke into my house?"

"Yes," he replies after a beat.

"That's… odd."

"Maybe," he hedges, and I wonder what he's talking-ing about.

"What do you mean maybe?" I wonder why I can't control the words that are coming out of my mouth.

Obviously, it must be the bottle of wine.

"With Rachel missing and everything going on with the bill and the blackmail," he explains, "I needed to make sure you were all right when you didn't answer."

Ahh, so it was a pity visit. That doesn't sting my ego at all. But that's fine. I shouldn't want him. Ryan Black has future heartache written all over him. Unfortunately, I know that heartache would come on the heels of some of the best orgasms I've ever had in my life. The world is cruel.

"Well, you can see I'm fine, so have a good night," I say before I turn to head to my closet to change into some pajamas. If I hadn't had so much wine, maybe I would've noticed he was following me into the closet and not showing himself out.

"We need to talk," he says as I slip my dress over my head and toss it in the hamper destined for the dry cleaners. He's seen everything already, and I'm drunk enough I don't really care, so I strip out of the rest of my clothes and pull on some lace-trimmed silk pajama pants and a matching camisole.

"What about?" I ask as I make my way into the bathroom and begin to wash the makeup off my face. He trails a single fingertip down my spine when I bend over the sink to rinse my face, and it's all I can do to keep my reaction from showing.

He answers me when I pat my face dry.

"Did you listen to my voicemail messages?" he

asks, changing the subject as I slip my earrings from my ears and place them in a little bowl on the counter.

"Some," I say, shrugging as I reach for my toothbrush but find myself spun around and my back pressed against the counter. "W-what?"

"I told you I was done fucking around."

"What does that even mean?"

"This," he says, and then he crashes his mouth down on mine, and when he opens, I cave to the pressure and he licks inside.

I melt against him. I never stood a chance. I know it, and so does Ryan. But I have to put a stop to this before he tramples my heart all over again.

"Ryan," I whisper when I pull back, and he lets me, but he also keeps me close.

"Julia."

"I can't risk it again," I whisper. "It hurts too much."

"I hurt you," he acknowledges. "And I'm so fucking sorry for that. But I'm going to show you that the fall is worth the risk."

"No."

"Jules—"

"No," I say, stronger this time. "I don't want that."

"It'll be good between us," he says. "You know that."

"I know it could be and probably would be," I reply. "That is, until you turn your anger on me again. And it will cut deep, and I know from experience I don't want to feel that again."

"Jules, if you'll just listen—"

"No," I say, interrupting him. "It's been a long day, and I need you to go."

"All right, I'll go," he concedes.

"I'll see you on Monday."

"You'll see me before then."

And then he turns on his heels, and I watch him walk out of my bathroom. I hear the door click closed behind him downstairs, and as I lie down in my bed, I wonder if I made another mistake.

THE RUMOR
MILL IS ON
FIRE WITH
TALK OF THE
PRESIDENT'S
FATHER READY

CHAPTER 3

I was literally bred, born, and raised for moments like this.

Where Grace had a normal childhood in the suburbs, I was born into one of the most prominent families in New York. When I was a tot, I studied classical ballet and piano. When I was old enough, I learned French, Spanish, German, and Japanese. I went to the best finishing school money could pay for. I earned top grades always, because anything less than a solid A was a failure and I would find myself grounded. I was accepted to NYU on my own merits and was recruited as a legacy into the sorority my mother and my grandmother were in.

I keep a fit figure through running and yoga. I do not overindulge in anything, because I was raised in a very strict regime in order to maintain a trim physique to best showcase haute couture. I actually love to run. It helps me clear my head on difficult days.

And I have done all of these things, lived this life, not because I wanted to, not because it filled some deep-seated need in me to be the best that I could be, but because it was expected of me. I was bred and raised by parents of the social elite, and my sole purpose was to make a match that would benefit the family business in some way.

I find it incredibly ironic that after over thirty years of being the best of the best, I'm seen as nothing but a failure and a disappointment to my parents.

"May I escort you in?"

I turn toward the voice that sets me on edge every single time. While there is a very specific protocol for entering this event, I do not need an escort in. I'm that important. I go to politely decline, but when I turn around, the president's father is there. He's standing entirely too close to me, and I take a startled step back. I lose my balance when I shift my weight too quickly on my incredibly tall and pencil-slim heels.

He wraps his arm around my waist and pulls me into his arms, his reflexes faster than I would have figured for someone his age. I hear a disgusted noise and turn my head to see Captain Black watching me. He must have seen the whole thing, and I feel heat hit my cheeks at my embarrassment.

"Thank you," I say quietly before pushing away from the senior senator, but it's too late. Ryan had already walked away.

"Always happy to help a beautiful woman in need," he replies with a wink and an inappropriate look at my breasts. I send him a tight smile, hoping he understands I will not be conquered, but I don't think he gets it. Especially when he continues. "And I'd be more than happy to help with your needs."

I kind of want to throw up in my mouth. It's not that he's twice my age or my friend's father-in-law. I could get past all those things if he was a good man, but I get the feeling that he's not. There's something about the way he looks at me that just makes me feel dirty. And I don't like it.

"Thank you, but I think I'm all right now," I say quietly and then turn on my toes and head off to find Cara. I know she thinks I've been assigned her babysitter for the evening, but in truth, she's become one of my dear friends, and I need her to deflect the senior senator's attention. I have a feeling he's going to be a problem.

I link her arm through mine once we're inside the ballroom, and we go off to find our table. Cara, obviously, is marked to sit next to Rick on one side and me on the other. There are several dignitaries and their wives and Captain Black around our table. I switch his place card with one a few seats down so that he's not sitting right next to me. It was a stupid thing to do, and there is no excuse other than I really need to look after Cara and do my job, and I'm not sure I could do what I need to with him looking down his nose at me all night.

I saw the way he looked at me when he thought I was flirting with the president's father, and it didn't make me feel good.

We take our seats, and I do my best to make small talk with everyone. I try to pull Cara into the conversation, but she's clearly uncomfortable, and I don't blame her. I can't imagine what she's going through. I feel Ryan's eyes on me through the whole dinner, but I don't give in to my urge to look at him.

After dinner, Rick takes Cara to introduce her to some people, and I make my way around the room for a bit. Unfortunately, the senator chooses that time to attack again.

"Can I buy you a drink?" he asks. His mouth is very close to my ear, his body presses close, and he places his hand at the small of my back just a little too low.

"I'm good. Thank you though," I say as politely as I can. While I'm not interested in getting screwed by the president's father, I still have to be courteous. This is a powerful man with powerful friends in this town. It wouldn't do me any good to piss him off.

And wounded male pride can be a real bitch.

"You know," he says, and I can feel his breath against my neck, "we would make a smart match."

I'm not sure that "smart" has anything to do with it. In fact, I'm not even sure what he's offering me right now. All I know is there's no way in hell. I'll relocate to Texas and teach civics at the high school my friend

Angie and her husband work at. There's a part of me that wants to run far and fast, because this man sets off my internal alarms.

"That's quite… flattering," I murmur for lack of anything more diplomatic. "But I'm not looking for anything right now."

He stares at me, and I hold his gaze, and while I do, I get the impression he knows I'm lying and wants me to know that he knows. Weaving a tangled web of romantic partners is not something I should be engaging in when there are much darker games at foot.

"I won't wait forever, Julia," he says to me, his voice low and full of warning, so much so that it makes the hair stand up on the back of my neck.

"And I wouldn't expect you to," I reply with steel infused in my own voice. "Now, if you'll excuse me."

I step away from him and don't look back as I wend my way through the crowd. I smile at people as I drift past them, but it does little to slow my racing heart. The senior senator is going to be a problem. I hoped I could evade his advances until he forgot about me, but that will clearly not be possible. Now more than ever, I remember that I made these choices. This is why I vowed to stay single. Men are nothing but trouble.

I keep moving through the crowd. I need to find someplace quiet to silence my thoughts before I can go back to Cara.

I step into the hall I know leads to the restrooms and keep moving. There are plenty of nooks and crannies and even a few secret tunnels here where I can find a moment to myself. The music is muted, and I can no longer hear the voices of the evening after I turn a corner.

"Are you going somewhere?" a deep voice growls in my ear as a strong hand wraps around my upper arm and pulls me through a door.

I am up to my eyeballs in highhanded men, and I'm beginning to think I've had enough.

"What do you want?" I let out a frustrated sigh. I feel like I'm spinning out of control, and I very much prefer being in the driver seat of my own life.

"Are you going to fuck him?" Ryan vibrates with his question.

"I'm not sure how that's any of your business," I reply. And as much as the idea bothers me, it's not Ryan's place to judge. He forfeited that right when he tossed nasty words at me and fled my house before he even had his pants buttoned up.

"You know he's old enough to be your grandfather," he says as he stares at me, and I force a bored expression across my face.

"Your concern is touching." I let my sharp words hang in the air.

"Does he get to touch you?" he asks as he brushes a lock of my hair behind my ear. "Do you let him suck your tits or eat your pussy? Are you wet for him like you are for me?"

"I think I hate you," I whisper.

"I don't think I care," he says, and then his mouth crashes down on mine.

As much as I said I didn't want him again after the way he left me before, it was all a lie. I know that now, and so does he, because we can both feel the way my body melts against his, the way my mouth opens under his, and the sound of my soft moan as he licks inside.

I never stood a chance.

"That's what I thought," his deep voice rumbles in my ear, and then he licks up the side of my neck and trails his lips over my cheek and behind my ear as he bunches my dress up in his hands. I help hold my full skirts as he traces his fingertip over the lace edge of my panties before he pulls them aside.

My breath sears in my lungs as he swipes a finger over my center. My cheeks burn with embarrassment, because we both know how wet I am for him now, and the smug look Ryan is giving me tells me that he's going to be unbearable afterward.

He kisses me again, and it's hard and hungry, wet and deep. I clutch his shoulders, and I'm unable to do anything more than just hold on.

But it's when he pulls back, taking his ruthless mouth away from mine, that my eyes flutter open. His dark eyes watch me intently, and then I gasp as he plunges a finger deep inside me. He watches me as he pumps his hand again and again before he slides his fingers out and swirls his fingertip over my clit, covering me in my wetness.

I begin to rock my hips against his hand. I can't help myself.

I need more.

Ryan plunges two fingers deep again, pumping them in and out of me in hard and fast strokes. He watches me, his eyes never leaving my face, and my breaths come out in pants as he drives me closer and closer to a precipice I'm unprepared to go over.

He drops his mouth to mine as he swirls his thumb over my clit, and my mouth drops open, but Ryan doesn't deepen our connection there. He quietly takes in my breaths and drinks down my whimpers. I hold onto him so tightly that my finger whiten with the pressure as he thrusts his fingers inside me over and over, and then everything stills and I come.

Ryan covers my mouth with his to stifle the noises I make as he slowly glides his fingers in and out. When I can't take it anymore, my flesh too sensitive for any more, I grip his forearm in my hand. He kisses my mouth once more then the corner and then places another on my cheek before he slips his fingers free, rights my panties, and pulls my skirt back down to cover me.

My breath saws in and out of my lungs, and I watch him with rapt attention as he licks his fingers clean. I want him still, even though he's just seen to me. I want to touch him, to please him, to make him lose control the way he makes me.

I start to drop to my knees to return the favor, but Ryan catches me under my arms to stop me. Rejection burns through me, and it is not a nice feeling.

"No, honey," he says softly. "This one was just for you."

"Okay," I whisper, even though I don't feel okay, but at this point I will say anything to get out of this closet, because we're developing a nasty habit of me giving my body to Captain Black and then him rejecting me shortly after. A habit I desperately need to break. And even as I think that, I know that if he came to me again, I still wouldn't say no, and I'm not sure what that says about me either.

"We should get back out there," he says as he watches me, and I get the distinct impression he sees more than I want him to.

"Yeah," I agree. The need to get out of here is growing inside me more and more. Ryan Black is a poison, and I'm afraid the only way to get rid of it is to work him out of my system. "I'll go first."

And then I scoot around him and scurry out the door. I stop at the ladies' room to make sure I don't look like I was just finger-fucked in a broom closet, and finally the stars shine on me, because I don't. And then I decide to go rescue Cara, when really I'm the one who needs the rescue.

"Mind if I steal your girl for a minute?" I ask Rick. I can see he wants to say no. I lower my voice and whisper for his ears only, even though I know Cara can hear me to, "She'll be safe. I promise. And Ryan is close."

His dark eyes flare, and then he answers, "Sure. Don't be gone too long." And then he places a hard but fast kiss to her lips before letting her go and turning away.

I thread her arm through mine and lead her to a darker corner of the room where people don't seem to be hanging around, grabbing each of us a glass of champagne from a passing waiter on the way by.

"How are you holding up?" I ask Cara as I pass her a glass.

"I think I'm doing all right."

"I know you're nervous, but you're doing marvelous!"

She looks scared shitless, and I should have been paying attention to her, but instead I was fucking off in a broom closet with my worst enemy. I'm an awful friend. I'm not going to let her out of my sight for the rest of the night.

"Really?" she asks incredulously. "Because it feels like I've said three words the whole night and only spoke when asked a question."

"Yes! That's exactly what the group wants," I say, rolling my eyes. "Women aren't supposed to speak."

"Then why are you?" she asks me as she sips her champagne and watches me, not with judgement but interest in what I have to say. She's so much like

Grace—easy to be around and kind—that I forget I haven't known her all that long.

"Because it irritates them."

"No, you do not."

"Oh, I totally do. Everyone knows it too," I reply as I sip my drink. It's true; I tired of being seen and not heard a long time ago. It's been years since I've let someone tell me how I should be. I'm good at my job, smart, strong, and successful, and anyone else can fuck off.

"And they just let you get away with it?" she asks me, sounding shocked but also a little in awe.

"Mostly," I answer with a shrug until Ryan catches my eye from across the room, and I feel my face pull into a frown. Ryan looks absolutely frustrated and more than a little murderous. And I don't fucking care. He is not going to be my problem anymore. If I just stay away from him, he'll go away, and then I can forget what it's like to have him master my body and dole out fantastic orgasms. "Well, except for Ryan. He doesn't seem to approve of me very much."

"I'm sorry," she whispers.

Don't be. I'm not." I shrug again.

"I like you, Julia Fairchild," Cara tells me, and I laugh. She's good people. "I'm keeping you."

"Oh good, because I've already decided to keep you too."

"Fantastic news." She smiles back before I catch

sight of Grace throwing up a smoke signal from across the room.

"Oh dear, Grace is sending up a Romeo."

"She's sending up a what?" Cara asks.

"See how she's sliding the pendant on her necklace back and forth while glancing over here every so often?"

"Yes, I do," she answers. "What is she doing? She looks a little ridiculous."

"She does, doesn't she?" I reply with a sigh. "She's sending up a Romeo. It's an old sorority secret. When you need an out, you slide your necklace like that, and a sister or two will come rescue you. Simple as that. So you see, it's our duty to go find out what our dear First Lady needs."

"Seeing how she's very pregnant and dancing a bit, I'm guessing it's the powder room," Cara says. I never would have thought about that, but then again, out of all three of us, I'm the only one who's never been pregnant, and I probably never will.

"It looks like you would be correct."

"We should probably hurry."

"Hello!" I say brightly, interrupting whatever the man she was speaking to was saying. "Will you excuse us for a moment? I need to steal the First Lady for some important business."

I don't even give him time to reply. I just smile dazzlingly, loop my arm through Grace's, and wheel her away with Cara in tow. I smile at everyone, as does Grace, and Cara follows our lead, but I do not slow as I move us through the room.

We bypass a ladies' room and travel farther down the hall. Grace's main agent follows us at a discreet distance. We take a turn down another hallway and find a more private restroom. A quick look shows that it's empty.

"Thank God. Jake's giant baby is Irish folk dancing on my now very teeny tiny bladder. I thought I was going to die," Grace exclaims as she rushes for a stall.

"Well, we're all glad you didn't." I laugh.

Grace comes out of the stall and washes her hands. As she's reapplying her lipstick, two women walk in the restroom, laughing and clearly enjoying themselves.

"Did you see the way Jake was looking at you?" one asks the other, and I recognize her. In fact, I'm wondering what the hell they're doing here. "He clearly can't wait to get his hands on you, and who could blame him? His wife is the size of a barn."

"And I can't wait for him to get his hands on me," Ashley Jeffries purrs. God, I cannot stand her. Either of them, really. "He's so good with his hands."

The door swings open, and they see us standing there. I know exactly what they're up to. We all know exactly what these two monsters are trying for.

"Oh!" Ashley gasps in mock horror. "You weren't supposed to hear that."

"You don't say," Grace drolls.

"I never wanted you to find out about us this way," she says, like Jake would actually want anything to do with her. Ashley was in the running for Grace's position as Jake's wife, or so she thought before Grace entered the picture. And there is no doubt where anyone is concerned that Jake is faithful to the wife he so openly adores.

"Sure, sure," Grace says.

"It's just that you know Jake and I have known each other for so long, and our families go way back. One thing just kind of led to another," she says. "You know how it is."

Her ridiculousness hangs in the air between us, and then I swear, I try, but I just can't help myself. A teeny tiny giggle escapes me. And then another. And another, until I'm bent over laughing so hard I can't catch my breath and tears are running down my face. Thank God for waterproof mascara!

"I don't see what's so funny," Ashley snaps.

"You are," I say, wiping a tear from my eye. "Like anyone would believe that load of horse shit that just spewed from your mouth. Everyone can see Jake is madly in love with his wife. You're just mad it's not you after the military campaign you waged last year for his ring. Right, Cara?"

"Right," she backs me up immediately. If there was a test you had to pass to get into the sisterhood, Cara just passed with flying colors when she helped me clearly defend the Team Grace camp. "Jake is full gone for Grace. Anyone can see that. The thought of him cheating is laughable at best. Good one."

"I wouldn't be so quick to laugh if I were you," she says, turning on Cara, and I hold my breath to see what kind of vitriol she's going to spew and how Cara will react to it. "Amy was talking to Rick earlier, and he was very interested. If you know what I mean."

"Oh, I do, and I'm not worried," she replies coolly, and I'm not gonna lie; she impressed the fuck out of me. I didn't know anyone else could swing around a pair of lady balls as big as mine. I stand corrected.

"We should probably get going, ladies," Grace says to us. "Nice seeing you again, Ashley."

"Don't think you'll keep him!" she whisper-shouts as we leave. "He will come back to me. He always comes back to me."

"Wow," Cara whispers. "What a bitch."

We wind our way back through the crowd, and Jake steals Grace away. Their duty for the evening is done, and he's obviously read to get Grace home safely. They're so sweet to watch.

"Ready to go?" Rick asks as he approaches Cara.

"I thought you'd never ask."

I laugh. Awe, young love. "Be good, kids," I tell them with a smile before I lean in and kiss Cara on the cheek. And then Rick leads her out with an arm around her.

I feel a warning tingle go up my spine, and I look back over my shoulder. Ryan is talking to someone from some dignitary's entourage, but he's watching me, and the look he's sending my way promises something ominous. So before he has a chance to do or say anything else that confuses me or makes me want something I shouldn't, something I know I can't have, I turn and run.

PRESS SECRETARY SHAKES THINGS UP AT WHITE HOUSE

CHAPTER 4

Hate myself

"Babe," the sexiest voice I've ever heard says, and I hate that it heats my body up from the inside out, even in my sleep. "We gotta talk."

"I don't wanna," I mumble, never opening my eyes, and I pull the covers up higher around my ears and let myself drift back to sleep.

I feel the covers slip down my body, and the cool night air tickles my back. My eyes pop open, and I take in the darkness of my bedroom late at night. I roll over and see Ryan sitting on the edge of my bed.

"What are you doing here?"

"We have to talk," he repeats. The corners of his mouth twitch like he finds something amusing, although I don't know what. What I do know is that I can't let him talk, because whatever the hell it is he wants to say to me in the middle of the night cannot be good. If it had to do with Rachel, he would have said it right out. But he mentioned when he had broken into my bedroom earlier that he wanted to talk.

I was humiliated when he walked out of my house the first time without a backward glance—not that one would have been welcome with the way he was snarling at me—after he fucked me on the foyer floor. He was hot one minute and then cold and harsh the next. Ryan taught me a lesson, one that should have sunk in through all my years of dating in New York: Men are rats.

Even though I feel in my gut that he's not. There's something about the way he is around everyone else. He's private, and no one really knows anything about him, but Jake trusts him with his life. He even told Grace, who told me. I just have this feeling there's more than meets the eye with Ryan Black.

So I can't let him explain why he was a jackass the other day, because if he shows me that he's a decent guy, I'll want to fall for him, and I can't let that happen. It hurt when I only had the promise of him and he threw me away. If he's a good guy and into me and then he throws me away again, it'll destroy me.

"Babe," he says, and I look at him watching me. I realize that my mind must've wandered off. "Did you hear me?"

Oh, I heard him all right. But that's all I'm going to hear tonight. In my sleepy brain, I figure I have two choices: fight it out with him, knowing he will talk circles around me and win, and then he will get to tell me all he wants to say and the whole thing will be moot. Or I can take matters into my own hands and distract him until I can get better locks installed on my house so he can't keep breaking in like this.

I'm pretty sure I'll realize this is a harebrained scheme that has no potential to work in the morning, but for now, I'm still a little champagne drunk and definitely a lot sleepy, so I don't think about it anymore. I just launch myself at Ryan, and he does not disappoint when he catches me.

I wrap my arms around his neck and press my lips to his. I may have started the kiss, but Ryan finishes it as he opens his mouth against mine and licks inside. His arms went tight around me when he caught me, but now he traces patterns up and down my back and then under my camisole, and it goes up and up and up then over my head.

"Ryan," I whisper as he looks into my eyes. Whatever he sees there, I don't know, but something comes over him. He changes before my eyes, and then he dips his head and draws my nipple into his mouth.

I squirm as he nips and kisses my breast before moving to the other, and when he sucks it into his mouth, my squirming turns to rocking over his lap. I feel his hard cock between my thighs and let out a whine as I use him to heat up my body.

I grab his T-shirt in my fists and push it up over his head, making him let go of my breast so I can take it off and throw it to the floor. With his hands on my ass, he puts a knee to the bed and tips me backward so I land on my back. And then he grabs the waist of my pajama pants and rips them down my legs.

He pushes my thighs open with his strong hands, and then his mouth is there on me. He doesn't go slow or tease, no. Ryan devours me. I run my fingers through the hair at the top of his head where it's longer and pull him closer to me as he sucks my clit deep into his mouth.

I'm seconds away from coming when he pulls back, and I wonder, for a split second, if this is some kind of punishment, to bring me to the edge and then back off. That is until I see his hands move to his belt buckle and I realize he's just getting down to the good stuff.

I let my eyes trail over him. His body is beautiful with lean, chiseled muscles all over that lead down to a long, hard cock that stands tall and thick from the opening of his jeans. He's so good-looking that he makes my breath catch. I might hate myself in the morning, but I'm going to let myself enjoy this right now.

Ryan covers my body with his, and I let out the breath I'd been holding when he slowly slides deep inside me. But this is definitely different. This isn't a hard and fast fuck on the entryway floor. This is slow and deep. Ryan looks deep in my eyes as he moves inside my body.

His mouth hovers over mine, and he touches his lips to mine every so often, but he doesn't let it deepen.

He doesn't close his eyes but instead watches me. I don't know what he's trying to say with his eyes, his mouth, and his body, and I don't want to either. This can lead to nothing but my heartache.

And still, I have no choice.

I rake my nails down his back as he plunges over and over. I gasp as he hits something deep inside me that makes my thighs tighten around his hips, and he moves faster, drives farther.

I open my mouth to cry out as the climax that Ryan had been carefully building washes over me, and he covers my mouth with his, giving me his deep rumble as he follows me over the edge.

Last time, he couldn't pull out and pull up his pants fast enough, but this time, he slowly glides in and out of me as the last trimmers of my orgasm roll over me. He traces the tip of his nose down the side of mine and places soft kisses on my mouth. It's sweet and it's intimate and it's too fucking much.

Oh my God, what have I done?

I put my open palms to the front of his shoulders and gently shove him back while I try to tamp down the stinging behind my eyes. Ryan rolls to his side, and I lose his cock. I feel a pang in my heart, but I don't stop. I push up from the bed and head toward my bathroom.

"Jules?" he asks.

"I was wrong," I whisper as I grip the doorjamb tight in my hands. "I can't do this."

"Julia," he says more firmly, and I can hear the rustle of the sheets, so I move fast into the bathroom.

"If you ever respected me, even a little bit, you'll leave," I whisper, and then I shut the door tight and twist the lock.

"Jules, honey, open the door," he says, and I can hear his hands against the wood panel. "Please, baby, we've gotta talk."

"I can't," I whimper, and I hate that I can hear myself cry. I fucking hate it, and I hate that he can hear it too.

"Please, Jules," he pleads. "I have to hold you."

"No!" I practically shout. "Go. You have to go."

"Julia."

"Please," I sob. "Just go."

There's silence around me that I fill with my cries, but I know he's still there, listening to me lose it. And then he says, "All right, honey. I'll go… for now. But this isn't over."

But he's wrong. We have to be over now.

I hear the rustle of fabric as he dresses, and then he says softly, "I'll talk to you tomorrow." And then he knocks softly on the door before I hear his boots move down the stairs.

I hold my breath until I hear the front door close, and then I give in to my tears and hysteria. I lie down on my fluffy lilac bathmat, and I cry myself to sleep, the whole time thinking I won't hate myself tomorrow, because I hate myself now.

How could I have been so stupid?

PRESIDENT'S AIDE-DE-CAMP INJURED IN HUNTING ACCIDENT

CHAPTER 5

I was wrong

My eyes burn and my face is puffy. As I stare in the bathroom mirror, I realize I am not a pretty crier. In fact, I look like absolute shit.

There's no way I can go out looking like this. Today, I'm going to have to do some serious self-care. I'm going to lock myself up and turn off my phone. I'll order takeout and watch Lifetime movies, because I'm not sure I could handle the happily ever afters of Hallmark in my current mental state. I need a day of murderous nannies and psycho stalkers. Maybe I'll dive into that tiger documentary everyone is talking about.

But first up is a hot shower. I turn the taps to steaming hot and climb in. My muscles ache from sleeping on a bathmat, and the hot water goes a long way to work them out. I finish rinsing off and then pat myself dry.

I pull on panties and a sports bra, because I'm going to be comfortable today, but I'm also not going to be photographed looking like a saggy-boobed psycho when I open the door for some Uber Eats. I pull on a worn soft pair of jeggings that are more legging than jeans and a couple layered tank tops in different colors. I top it all with my favorite NYU sweatshirt that's been worn and washed so much that it's soft and cozy.

I dry my hair and twist it up into a messy bun on top of my head and dab a light amount of makeup on my face. I hate this step, and it seems stupid, unless you've been caught looking like you're seven hundred years old because your hair and makeup isn't done, which I have, and that was not a fun box to check. So I layer a tinted moisturizer and powder with a soft, dewy pink blush. I swipe some dark brown mascara on my lashes, and then I cap the tube and toss it back in my bathroom drawer.

I make my way downstairs and pop a pod in my Keurig as it makes the noises it does while it heats up. I place a cup on the little tray all while dreaming about the hot liquid that will magically help me get my life in order, because, real talk, something has to change. I can't keep going on like this. Maybe it's time I throw in the towel and go back to New York. I could always let my mom marry me off to someone with powerful business connections to further the family business. It would suck, but maybe I wouldn't feel so alone.

Or I could go to Texas and visit my friend Angie and her family. We were college roommates. She,

Grace, and I stayed close, even though life took her to East Texas through a series of unfortunate life events, but she found her happy in the form of a retired professional football player and their daughter.

Then again, her husband Cody has the same slow southern drawl Ryan does, and I don't know if I could handle the reminder of his sexy voice every day.

Life sucks.

I'm just about to lower the little lid to brew my coffee when there's a knock at the front door. I let out a frustrated groan. I just wanted one day to get myself in order. Is that too much to ask?

Apparently, it is, because there's another knock at the door. I let go of the little handle and make my way to the front door. I twist the lock and pull the door open and instantly regret I did.

"Mornin', honey," Ryan says as the corners of his mouth tip up in a smile.

"What do you want?"

"Aren't you going to let me in?" he asks, and if his booted foot wasn't blocking the door, I'd have already shoved it closed.

"Not if I can help it," I mutter, making his smile widen.

"You don't mean that," he replies with a sexy rumble to his voice.

"If I don't let you in, will you just break in later?"

"Probably." He chuckles. "But this is business."

"Rachel?" I ask.

"Something like that," he says. "Let me in and I'll tell you."

"This better not be a trick," I warn as I slowly step back to open the door wider to allow him entrance.

"Donovan wants everyone to rally around Cara, because she's falling apart," he says instantly as soon as the door closes.

"What can I do?" I ask.

"Grab your purse," he replies. "We're all heading to his place."

"I'll follow you." I try to avoid spending too much time in Ryan's company. This way, I can beg off early.

His smile widens. "No."

"Oh fine," I snap as I grab my bag off the counter and slide my feet into a pair of ballet flats.

Ryan follows me through the house and takes my keys from me when I move to lock the door and does it for me. He unlocks his truck and opens the passenger door for me before closing it once I'm settled. And then he walks around with a smirk on his face that I'm choosing to ignore, and he climbs up into the driver seat.

He heads to the next town over, one a little more family friendly than mine, and we stop to pick up some coffee and donuts before heading on over to Rick's house, where he has coordinated this well-planned attack to distract Cara.

"We brought takeout," Ryan says as we let ourselves into the house that's already brimming with our friends.

"And coffee," I add with a big, fat fake smile on my face. "Lots and lots of coffee."

"What's all this?" Cara asks, and Grace cringes. Grace never could keep a poker face around the people she loves. Cara clearly knew nothing about this planned visit, and Grace just spilled the beans.

She swipes at her temples, and I can tell she's hanging on by a very thin thread, so I ask, "Can I get you a cup of coffee, honey?"

"No," she says just a little too sharply. "I have a headache. I think I had just a little too much champagne last night."

"Okay, but—"

"I'm just going to go lie down," Cara inserts. "Let me know if you need me."

And then she scurries up the stairs. I look to Grace, who has a concerned look on her face. I feel the same way. Cara is falling apart, and there's nothing we can do to stop it.

"Any news?" I ask softly, and Jake just shakes his head.

"Maybe we should go check on her," Grace suggests. "Maybe the crowd was overwhelming but she'd want some company. Come with me, Jules."

"Okay."

We make our way up the stairs, tiptoeing softly like a bunch of crappy cat burglars. Grace tries the door handle, and it rattles but doesn't turn. Cara has locked the door. Shit. That can't be good.

"It's locked," Grace whispers before knocking lightly.

"Honey, are you all right?" Rick asks softly from behind us.

"Do you think she's okay?" Grace asks him.

"She'll be fine," he answers tersely. "She's probably just sleeping. It was a late night last night."

"But don't you think we should have told her…." Grace's voice trails off.

"What's going on?" I ask.

"Absolutely not," Rick says. "She has enough on her mind."

"But Rick—"

"Just leave it alone," he snaps.

There's not much we can do, so Grace and I do as Rick asks and let it go.

We make our way back downstairs, where everyone is sipping coffee and waiting. A ballgame plays low in the background, but I couldn't tell you who is playing or what sport. That's how high tensions are right now. When Rick, Jake, and Ryan devised a plan to bait the kidnappers last night, I was worried, now I'm terrified.

"We should have heard from them by now," Rick

says, and I can hear the frustration in his voice.

"We will," Ryan assures calmly. "You have to let the plan work." After a moment, he turns in his seat. "Did you hear that?" Ryan asks. He's suddenly alert, and it's creepy the way he does that, but it also stands the hairs on my arms on end.

"Hear what?" Rick's brow furrows.

"It sounded like the door opened," he says, reaching for his gun that's tucked into the back of his jeans. "I'm just going to go check that out."

"Sure," Rick says.

This is all so crazy. I'm not sure what to do with myself, but I know I need to stay calm for my friends. Otherwise, I don't know. But I hate this.

"Hey, Rick?" Ryan calls out from the back of the house, and I instantly know something is wrong.

"Yeah?" Rick calls out.

"The side door is unlocked."

Rick jumps up and runs upstairs. I can hear doors opening and closing, and I know—we all know.

"She's gone."

I grab Grace's hand, and she squeezes mine tight as the men follow him upstairs. We wait silently while they speak in low tones I can't hear upstairs. And then they all file down the stairs and out the door.

"Stay with Grace," Jake barks as he follows them out.

"I guess we're supposed to stay here," she says.
"I'll make some coffee."

FUNERAL PLANS ARE PENDING

CHAPTER 6

Little white lies

"It's time to move," Gus, Jake's Secret Service Agent, says.

"What's happening?" Jake asks.

"The package has been retrieved," Gus replies, tapping the earpiece in his ear. "We need to return to the residence."

"And Black?" Jake prompts, and I hold my breath, wondering what the hell could have happened to Ryan.

About an hour ago, everyone went tearing through the house while issuing orders for me to stay behind with Grace, so that's what I did. We hunkered down in the living room and waited. Sometime later, Jake and Gus returned. But that was it. Everyone else was gone, and the boys weren't talking.

"Gunshot wound." That was all he said. Just two

little words and all the breath whooshes out of my lungs.

"Status?" Jake barks.

"Alive," Gus replies before his eyes twitch over me for a split second, and I get the feeling there's a whole conversation happening between Gus and Jake just through looks and nods.

Someone shot Ryan. He's breathing, but I don't know how freely he's able to do so. God, was it only last night I swore I would never let him into my bed again? How stupid am I? I let my feelings get in the way once again, and now, some of the last memories I made with him are tainted, when I should have just been his friend.

And now I might never get the chance.

If I could go back in time, I would take every moment he came to me and let him love me well. I would gratefully accept every time he spoke to me with the sharp side of his tongue and not snap back. I would accept him for the man he is and not butt heads against it.

But now, all there can be done is to sit and wait.

I sit back on the sofa and curl my legs underneath me on the sofa. Grace curls her round form into Jake's side, and I watch with unchecked longing as he wraps his arm around her while he talks to Gus. The way they offer comfort to each other is beautiful to watch, and I want it for myself with everything that I am. Not Jake, but someone who wants to comfort me and care for me in times of need.

I have no idea how much time passes, and then the door opens, and Rick walks in with Rachel in one arm and his free hand holding Cara's.

I jump up, waiting for them to tell me what to do. I feel so helpless. Jake gingerly lifts Grace to her feet before gracefully gaining his own. He shakes Rick's hand, patting him on the back before turning to kiss Cara's cheek.

"Black?" I hear Jake ask, and Cara bites her bottom lip as tears well in her eyes. My heart goes out to my friend, but I'm also dying to know where Ryan is.

"He was shot." She sniffles.

"I know, honey," Jake replies.

"It was my fault."

"No," Rick bites out.

"He's right," Jake says. "Ryan did what he was going to do, what I knew he was going to do."

Rick shoots Jake a pointed glare that says they're going to talk later, but for now, he's letting it go. Clearly, Jake had all the plans, while everyone else only had bits and pieces.

Jake's phone rings, and he pulls it out of his pocket. "Alexander," he whispers to Rick and Gus, who seem to know what he means.

"Hello?" Jake answers.

"What the fuck is going on?" I hear a man's voice roar, and Jake moves to the other room.

"I should take her upstairs," Cara says, and lifts her

hands to take Rachel.

"I'll be there in a minute," Rick replies as he transfers the weight of his eight-year-old daughter from his arms to her mother's.

"I'll keep you posted," Jake says as he pockets his phone before turning to Rick. "Where is he?"

"Bethesda Memorial," Rick answers, and I realize they're talking about Ryan. He's in the hospital.

"If the press reach out," Jake says, turning to me, "he was injured in a hunting accident. He's taking time to recover but will be back on duty soon."

"So he's well?" I ask and realize that one question showed more about my true feelings than I intended, and I instantly want to pull the words back into my mouth. One glance at the gentle but concerned looks Rick and Jake are now both wearing tell me all I need to know. And it's not good.

"We don't know much," Rick says gently. "He's still at the hospital."

"Sure, sure," I say quickly. Too quickly. "I'm just trying to form my plan of attack." I can see no one believes me, but that's fine.

"I'll have Grace call you when I know more," Jake assures.

"Sure," I respond. "I should go."

"I'll have Gus drop you off on the way," he says. "We should be going too."

"My car—" I start to say, but then I realize Ryan

picked me up this morning and how weird it was that he showed up all sweet and friendly on my doorstep after he hit it and quit it—again—last night. "That would be appreciated."

"Of course."

"I can get a cab or an Uber if it's too far out of your way."

"It's no problem," Jake says. "Shall we?"

"Of course."

Grace and I follow Gus and Jake out to the car, and he opens the door. We all file in before Gus closes it behind us. He climbs in the passenger seat, and the driver takes off.

I sit silently in my seat while we ride. The sun is setting, and it glows a beautiful muted orange and pink through the tinted windows of the car. I see Grace turn to me a couple times out the corner of my eye, but I don't react. I just pretend like I don't notice her.

I hold in my sigh of relief when we pull into my driveway—just barely. I somehow manage to hold it together and not fling open my door and run screaming from the vehicle and into the night—again, just barely.

Gus steps from the front passenger seat and opens my door for me.

"Thank you," I say to him quietly before turning to the other occupants of the backseat. "Thanks for the lift. I'll see you Monday."

"I'll call you if I hear any news," Grace says gently, and the way she watches me makes me nervous. I know she sees more than I want her to. I'm good at holding in my emotions. I have to because of my job and who I am. But with Grace, it's like everything is laid bare. "Are you going to be all right?"

"Of course. Why wouldn't I be?" I ask and pray she doesn't call me out while I stand on the curb in front of my best friend's husband, who just so happens to be the president of the United States, and his secret service agents.

"Just wondering," she says, eyeing me suspiciously.

Gus shuts the door behind me and walks me to my front door. I pull my keys out of my purse and let myself in.

"Thanks again, Gus."

"Any time, ma'am."

The heavy front door shuts behind me with a thud. The click from the latch sounds throughout the quiet room, and I stand there, staring at the cold marble floor where Ryan fucked me and left, as I wait for the sound of the president's car pulling safely away.

I had thought, for the briefest of moments, that maybe he could be mine. I was so hurt and angry after he left me. And when he came back to me again and again, I still knew he wasn't for me to keep, and I let him have me anyways.

And as always, I was angry afterward.

But now I'm scared.

No. I'm not scared. I'm terrified. I'm terrified I'll never see his smile when someone says something he finds amusing, even if it's almost never me who does it because I frustrate him beyond belief. And I'm terrified I will never see the hungry look in his eyes when he wants me, that I'll never feel the way he makes my body melt into his hard one.

But most of all, I'm terrified I'll never get the chance to tell him how sorry I am that I disappointed him, that I couldn't be all he wanted me to be, because I learned the hard way a long time ago that I can only be me and no one else.

Finally, I drop my bag on the table under the big gilt-framed mirror in the entryway. There's a large copper bowl at one end, and a tall crystal vase full of fresh cut flowers at the other end. My purse, I often set in between. I fish out my phone from its depths, make sure the ringer is on as loud as it goes, and set it down.

My hands shake and my legs feel weak. My heart is racing, and I don't feel so good. I haven't had a panic attack in a long time. Now isn't the best timing for one, but they never seem to come when the time is right anyway.

I don't want to take medication, because I need to be alert when Grace phones with news, so I make my way into the kitchen and hold the kettle under the tap to fill it. I place it on the burner to heat while I pull down a mug and drop my favorite tea bag into the cup with the string and tag hanging perfectly down the side.

What I could really use is two Xanax and half a bottle of chilled chardonnay, but that's not going to happen.

When the whistle on the kettle blows, I jump and then turn off the burner while trying to force my heart rate to slow down. My hand shakes as I tip the kettle to pour the water into my mug, and I have to brace it with the other. I'm sure I look like a ridiculous adaptation of an actor on a cop show.

I set the kettle back on the stove and wait for my tea to steep. It's hot. I could never drink anything that was steaming hot, so not only will it need to steep, but it will also need to cool down after that. This, I know, will take some time.

So I pace.

I have to move my body when there is this much nervous energy bouncing around inside me like a bunch of demented pinballs in a broken machine that won't reset. So I walk all around the ground floor of my home.

I check my phone what seems like a million times, and there is not one message or missed call about Ryan. There is one from Grace though.

GRACE: Are you all right?

ME: Fine, why wouldn't I be?

I don't want her to worry about me, so I keep it vague. She doesn't need any more stress in her life. While I have never had one, I'm sure it can't be good for the baby. I would never forgive myself if something happened to Grace or the baby because of me.

> ME: Go relax. Stress can't be good for my godchild. Go read that baby book you love so much.

> GRACE: You're an asshole. You know how much I hate that book.

> ME: I do know, and I also know I'm your asshole.

> GRACE: That you are.

> ME: Go away.

> GRACE: Fine. Call me if you need me.

> ME: I will.

I won't. I'm pretty sure we both know it too. But that's all right. I'll be fine, because I always am.

I grip my phone in my hand. It's been well over an hour, and even longer since Rachel was rescued and Ryan was shot. What the fuck is going on? And why haven't we heard anything? I'm pretty sure that if something happened—good or bad—Grace would have phoned. She's my person. She wouldn't let me down. Actually, I know for a fact that if Ryan died, Grace would be here to hold me while I cried and mourned the man who would never be mine but who I care for anyway. Her team of secret service agents would look on uncomfortably, because Grace knows, even if I've never shared the words with her of the complicated emotions I feel for him. She would do whatever was needed if I were headed for a crash of that magnitude. So he's not dead. *Thank God.*

But still, I have to know.

So I drop my phone in my bag and scoop out my car keys before running to the garage. I open the garage door, jump in my car, and drive like a tasteful bat out of hell toward the hospital. It wouldn't do for me to get arrested for reckless driving. The Associated Press would just love that.

I pull into the parking lot, unsure where to go, so I park by the emergency room and walk as quickly as I can through the automatic doors and straight to the desk.

"Can I help you?" the nurse asks me, and I freeze. There is no way in hell they are going to give me the information I need, so I do the only thing I think of on the spot, which is undoubtedly the wrong thing to do. I lie.

"Yes. My boyfriend was injured earlier today in a hunting accident, and I was told he's here."

She looks at me for a long time and must see something in me that she can trust, which is both wonderful and horrifying at the same time. The panic inside me is still welling up. I need to know Ryan is okay. Until the, I'm drowning in it.

"He went into surgery a little while ago," she says softly, and my heart seizes in my lungs. Surgery. Oh God, it's worse than I thought. She takes in the tears welling in my eyes and continues. "He should be out soon. You can go through those doors to the elevator and take it to the fifth floor. Heddie is the nurse there. She'll have more info for you."

"Thank you!" I say before I run for the doors. She pushes the button to unlock them right as I hit it and push through.

I take the elevator to the fifth floor like she said and push through another heavy door with a little rectangular glass window in it into another waiting room. There aren't many people, but it also isn't empty. There's an older man holding a purse and a jacket in his lap. And then there's a woman, probably ten years older than me, who's beautiful with short, no-nonsense blonde hair and fair skin with just a few attractive wrinkles by her eyes. With her are two teenagers. The girl sits with the woman while the boy stands. He looks at me for a second, and then I look away.

"Hello, can I help you?" the nurse who I assume is Heddie asks, and since my little white lie downstairs worked, I try it again up here, thinking I'll get the same results, but boy am I wrong. I would never have imagined how wrong I would be.

"Yes," I answer with confidence I should not feel. "My boyfriend was injured in a hunting accident earlier. I was told he was up here in surgery."

She looks at me for a moment, and I'm hoping she doesn't realize who I am. That's always a possibility when your face is on C-SPAN and every cable news outlet only every damn day. "And your boyfriend's name?"

"Ryan Black."

I am so wrapped up in my own panic that I don't feel the tension of the room go wired. I should have. I'm good at reading a room, and that's no lie. But this time, I don't feel it. I'm too driven for my need to find out if he's all right. I need to see it with my own eyes.

"What did you say?" the teenage boy asks from across the room, and I freeze.

"Nothing," I say, turning to him with a gentle smile on my face. "I'm just trying to find out some information about someone. I'm sorry to have disturbed you."

I should have noticed that the beautiful blonde and her daughter turned to look at me as well. Or that the nurse was looking a little nervous just now. I don't take in any of these things. Instead, I press on with my harmless white lie like an idiot.

"Did you say Ryan Black?" he asks. They might recognize his name. It's no secret the president's aide-de-camp is named Ryan Black. It's also a common first and last name, so who knows. Either way, I don't think twice about answering.

"Yes, why?"

"Because this is his wife and children," the nurse answers before the boy has a chance to. "I was trying to find a way to tell you, but sometimes ripping off the Band-Aid is best, child."

"I'm sorry?"

"He's my dad," the boy says kindly, not angrily.

"You're his girlfriend?"

"Umm…"

"My name is Caleb, but most people call me Cabe," he says gently like he's talking to a spooked animal, and he takes a slow, intentional step toward me. And then another.

"I think there's been some kind of a mistake," I whisper.

"I don't," he says, and I see now that his dark eyes and hair frame a face still a little soft with the last bit of youth, but this almost-a-man undoubtedly was born to Ryan. Shit. I need to leave. "I'd like to talk to you."

"I think I should go."

"No!" he says sharply. "Don't do that."

"I'm so sorry," I say on a sad smile. "I intruded, and I didn't mean to."

"Lacy, go get Dad," Caleb says to the girl, and now it's my turn to shout.

"No! Don't do that, honey," I reply, softening my tone. "I'm so sorry."

"Lacy, go," he says again. His eyes never leave mine.

"No, no, there's no need to do that."

"Lacy, baby, I think you should go get your daddy," the blonde says, and my eyes swing to hers. "Now."

She doesn't look angry, more inquisitive, and she speaks in a melodic twang that's a softer version of

Ryan's. It breaks my fucking heart, because I know without a doubt this beautiful woman and their two gorgeous children belong to Ryan like I never would.

"Let's just talk," her handsome son says as his sister gets up and pushes through the door. I swing my head back to look at him, and I feel my panic surge to new levels.

One thing is certain, and I should have been paying attention to my gut, because it's never steered me wrong before. I don't belong here, and we all know it. I refuse to step farther into the room and sit down to talk—or worse, wait for Ryan who is apparently fine to come and set me straight in front of his beautiful family. God, now I know why he was so angry after he took me. He didn't want to, because he has a family at home waiting for him.

The truth slaps me in the face.

In all the things I have said and done in my life to get where I am now, I never compromise my morals. I grew thick skin, and I can take a heavy dose of criticism, but never, not ever did I lower my standards. That is until I let Ryan Black fuck me on the marble floor of my foyer and I became the other woman.

I feel sick to my stomach.

"Dad will be here in a second," the girl says when she pushes back through the doors.

I can't believe this happened. This isn't me. This is not who I am, and if I'm anything, I will stop this right now. So I do the only thing I can.

"I'm so very sorry," I say softly, letting out the full meaning of the words I'm feeling for what I've done. "I shouldn't have come here."

And then I turn and run.

"Wait!" the blonde with the tinkling bell voice shouts, but I push through the doors. I hit the button for the elevator again and again. God, please let the doors fucking open. "Caleb, do something."

And then praise Jesus and all the baby angels, the elevator doors slide open, and I practically jump inside, hitting the button for the ground floor as I do. Ryan's son is there just as the door is about closed, and I will never for as long as I live forget the sad expression on his face that says just how sorry he is that this is happening.

"Don't do this!" he shouts, and then he's gone.

I don't wait to find out what happens next. I run out of the elevator, through the emergency room, and out to my car long before Ryan, his son, or any other member of their beautiful family can find me and tell me what an awful person I am.

I jump in and pull out of the lot, not sure where to go. I don't want to go home, so I drive around for the longest time. My phone rings over and over in the seat next to me, but I don't answer it. I pull into a fast food drive-thru and get more junk food than I should. I already feel sick, so this won't change that.

It'll only make it worse, voice tell me, but I ignore it.

But as I drive away with my greasy paper sack, I find I'm not really hungry at all. I sip my shake on the way home, pull into my garage, and park my car. I toss the takeout bag on the counter and chuck my shake cup in the trash. I open the fridge and pull out an open bottle of wine. Pouring it in a glass, I then tuck the bottle under my arm before scooping up my paper sack and walking into the dark living room. I set my bounty on the coffee table and plop down onto the couch.

I don't bother to switch on the lights, but I do turn on the television to an old movie channel. It's a black-and-white flick, and you can just tell it's not going to have a happy ending. Thank God. I don't think I could handle that right now.

I hear my phone ringing in the kitchen where I dropped my purse, but I let it ring. Who cares anyway?

I drink half the glass in one big sip and let it swirl in my brain for a bit. And then I set down my glass and pick up my burger. I manage to eat half of it, but I can't eat more than that, so I toss it back into the bag and roll it up, destined for the trash.

I drink another glass of wine while I watch the movie wrap up a tragic end that I can't seem to feel anything for, because I just feel so numb.

I pick up the empty bottle and my glass in one hand and the detritus from my dinner in the other and walk back into the kitchen. I put the glass in the sink and the garbage in the trashcan and recycling before shutting off the lights. Then I head back into the living room, switch off the TV, and head upstairs.

I know there's no way I can sleep tonight, but still, I should try. I have a big day tomorrow. Somewhere between the deep love the two main characters felt for each other and when the hero drove his car off a cliff, I decided to go on safari in Africa indefinitely. I watched a Bear Grylls show the other night and found it fascinating. Tonight, it sounds like a great life plan. So tomorrow, I'll give Jake my resignation and then get lost, and if my luck prevails, I'll be eaten by a hippo by this time next week.

Hope prevails.

I make my way up the stairs, still not bothering to turn on any lights, and head to my bedroom at the back of the house overlooking the backyard. I turn to my dressing table, pull off my sweatshirt, and kick off my sneakers. I'm not going to get ready for bed other than just falling in it, leggings and tanks and all, but not my bra. I reach under the hem behind my back and pulls it up over my head easily before sliding it out from the arm hole of my shirt.

"So boyfriend, huh?" someone says from behind me. "I haven't been one of those in a long fucking time."

And just like in the old movie I watched, I let out a scream worthy of Janet Leigh.

NEW SOCIAL
MEDIA POLLS
SHOW FAIRCHILD
'HOTTEST' PRESS
SECRETARY OF
ALL TIME

CHAPTER 7

"Come here," Ryan says as he lounges back on my bed. I press my palm to my heart to try to slow its fast beat that threatens to burst out of my chest. His eyes lower from my face to my breasts and heat. But I can't let this happen.

"What are you doing here?"

"Isn't it obvious?" he asks.

"Not to me."

"Come here," he repeats, and I swear my body wants to go to him even though I know I shouldn't. I can't. I cannot allow myself to be that woman.

"I met your wife," I blurt out and wish I hadn't because of how much vulnerability it shows. Ryan has this hold over me, and we both know it.

He sighs and runs the hand of the not-bandaged

arm through his dark hair. "Ex-wife."

"That's not what I heard," I mutter.

"Well, you would have if you hadn't ran away," he says. "And you'd have met her husband, Alan. Great guy. Civilian. He's in IT."

"IT?"

"Yeah, tech guy," he explains. "A real computer nerd."

"A nerd?" I ask stupidly, because I'm so surprised by the idea that Ryan and the beautiful blonde aren't together. They belong together. They fit in such a perfect way with their gorgeous dark-haired, almost grown children.

"Come here, honey, and I'll tell you about it," he says gently.

"I don't think I should."

"Why not?" he asks casually, and I don't think; I just respond, and I do it honestly.

"Because I lose my head when you're in close proximity."

"I happen to like you when you lose your head in close proximity to me," he replies with a smug expression playing about the corners of his mouth.

"You would," I mumble.

"But I'd also like to explain to you the order of events that led to the demise of my sixteen-year marriage to my high school sweetheart," he says. "And I'd like to hold you while I do it."

"Okay," I agree, because what else do you say to something like that? So I take a hesitant step toward him. And then another. And another until I'm standing right next to my bed.

"Come here," he says one last time, holding his good arm out, and I curl into his side. "Now, it's story time. Are you ready?"

"No," I answer honestly, and I feel his mouth smile against my head as he holds me close.

"Well, I'm going to tell you anyway."

"I figured as much."

"I was two years older than Kristen, two grades ahead of her in school. And even though we were young, I knew I was going to marry her," he says, and I feel something ugly curl in my belly. "That could have been the hormones, but I knew, so I married her the second she graduated and not a moment later. And I moved her into married student housing at A&M. I worked my ass off to graduate a year early, and I was already committed to the Marines. After that, we moved constantly with each new billet. And then came Caleb, who you met. Two years after that, Lacy."

He said it all like that explained everything, when in actuality, it explained nothing, and I'm left with more questions than answers. Questions I would not now, nor ever, give a voice to, because it isn't my business, but also because it might just break my heart.

"I was deployed," he continues, and I can't help but feel like this is where the fairy tale turns into a nightmare. "Kristen was getting tired of being a full-time single parent with a husband who was never there. I had thought things were fine. She sent the kids back to Texas to be with our families and said she had to work, and she did, but really she was having an affair—not with Alan, but some office douche."

I glance up at him, expecting to find pain in his eyes, but his face is completely void of emotion.

"One day, when I finally got the chance to call home, she broke down and told me. I wished for a long time after that she hadn't, because it changed everything. We were broken. I came home, and we tried, but I couldn't. I would lie in our bed with her at night, and when she turned to me, I would wonder, did he touch her like I did? Did he kiss her neck like I did? And I couldn't. We were broken, but not because of her affair. We were broken long before that when we let things get to the point that she would turn to someone else."

"I'm sorry," I say for lack of anything better.

"Me too," he says, squeezing his arm tighter around me for a second. "I won't say it was the best for a while, but we're still friends, and we managed to raise great kids. Alan works for himself, so when I said I had the opportunity for this job, they all signed on to follow me to D.C."

"That's nice."

"It's nicer than nice," he agrees. "We're a team, and it works."

"I'm glad you have that," I tell him, my voice soft.

"I'm glad you like that for me, honey," he says, and I think story time is over when he turns the tables on me. "Now, let's talk about what drove you to the hospital scared to death tonight."

"Story time is over," I reply, trying to pull away.

"All right, darlin'," he concedes, and his Texas twang is more pronounced than normal. "I'll let you make that play… for now, and we can move on to more… pleasurable pastimes."

"What?"

"I might need a little help getting undressed though."

"You can't be serious!" I practically shout. "You were just shot!"

"It's not as bad as it looks," he says as he begins to shrug out of his T-shirt. "It's just a little bit more than a flesh wound."

"I'm not so sure about that," I mumble as I watch him reveal his tan skin and muscle inch by gorgeous inch. "They said you were in surgery."

"I had to get a little patched up. They didn't even need to put me under," he says. "You're going to have to do all the work though."

"Do you really think we should be doing that right after you've been shot?"

"Baby, you are exactly what I should be doing right after I get shot."

I gasp. "What's that supposed to mean?"

"It means that after the shitty day I've had, I want to something sweet to get the taste of all the ugly out of my mouth," Ryan says, and he says it looking directly at me. "And that something sweet is you."

"Me?" I whisper.

"Yeah," he replies. "Now take off your clothes."

"W-w-what are you going to do?" I stammer, because even injured, Ryan's power and strength emanates from him in waves that fill the room and make me want to do what he asks me to.

"I'm going to lie back here on these pretty silk pillows of yours with all the frills in your girly bed, and you're going to sit on my face while I eat you," he says calmly, and by the glimmer in his eyes, I can tell he knows he's got me. My heart, which had calmed down, is racing again, and with just a few words, he has me clenching my thighs together and my panties wet.

"And then what?" I whisper, and his smile widens.

"And then you're going to ride my cock until we both come." And I have to admit I like the sound of that. "And then we're going to fall asleep in this bed. That is, unless you have other plans."

"I was going to go on a safari," I stupidly blurt out.

"Where to?" Ryan asks casually.

"Africa."

"For how long?"

"Forever," I admit, wondering why I can't get my

mouth to cease talking, and Ryan throws back his head and laughs. He must have scrambled my last remaining brain cells with his dirty talk.

"Baby?"

"Yeah?"

"Take off your clothes before I tear my stitches taking them off for you."

"Okay."

"Now would be good."

My hands shake as I stand and reach for the hem of my tank tops and pull them over my head. I hear Ryan groan as they drop to the floor before I dip my fingertips into the waistband of my leggings, push them down my legs with my panties, and step out of them when they hit the carpet.

I stand in front of him bare and unsure of what to do, which seems ridiculous. This isn't our first time together, but it is the first time I've ever had to take the lead. Before, I was always content to sit back and let Ryan set the tone, but now I can't help but feel like maybe things are changing, and I won't know just yet if it's for worse or for better.

"Come here," his deep voice rumbles, and I take a step closer. Ryan reaches out with his good arm and takes my hand in his, pulling me close before he places my palm over his crotch and covers my hand with his. He presses down so I can feel the heat and the hardness of him and how much he wants me. "Take my pants off."

He squeezes my hand over him once more before letting me go. Carefully, I hook my fingers in the front of his jeans and pop the first button and then the next and then the one after that until the neat row of buttons are all undone and I part the worn denim. I swallow as I stare at his miles of tan skin and the dark hair that lightly covers his chest, along with dog tags hanging around his neck. Before, I was with pretty men who preen like peacocks, but lounging in front of me now is a real man. It's like always having owned house cats and then accidentally letting in a lion.

"Quit playing with me, baby," he says, and my eyes snap up to meet his. They flicker and spark with an electrical current, and I want to dive into it with my whole body.

I dip my fingers into the waistband of his jeans and feel the heat from his skin where it touches the back of my hands as I drag his pants and boxer briefs down his muscular legs. The dark material slides over the heavy bulge between his legs, and then his cock springs free. It's long and thick and heavy as its veiny length bobs against his taut belly.

He's beautiful in a rough and rugged kind of a way, but I still don't stop until his clothes hit the carpet and he's left in nothing but his dog tags. He digs his heels into the bed and uses his powerful legs to propel his body down the bed. And when he settles, I place a knee to the bed next to him and then the other.

With his free arm, he grabs my hand and pulls me to move up the bed. Ryan guides me to a spot near his shoulders, and I'm not sure I can do this. I might die of embarrassment.

"Put your hands on the headboard," he commands, and I grip the iron curls at the top of the bed as he motions for me to place a knee on either side of his head. "Now lower down."

My bare pussy hovers over his mouth, and my body goes solid. I couldn't move if I wanted to, and I definitely want to, because I don't know how to be this woman. In the real world, I can demand and take what I want, but here in the now, with Ryan in my bed, I'm not sure I can.

Before I can put any more thought to it, Ryan grips my hip in his hand and arches up as he licks up my center, making me gasp.

"Come to me," he rasps as he drops back down to the bed, taking me with him.

"Ryan," I pant as he holds me tight to his face. He drives his tongue deep inside me before he rolls my clit deep into his mouth.

My fingers whiten where they grip the headboard as he devours me. He growls as I roll my hips in time with his ministrations, and I feel it rumble through me like thunder.

"Yes," I breathe as I arch my back.

I'm close. I'm so close, but as amazing as this feels, I don't want it like this. Ryan could have died today, and by some miracle he didn't. I could let him make me come like this, or I could come with him deep inside me.

"Ryan," I rasp as I pull up higher on my knees. He grabs me by my hip and pulls me back down to his mouth to take another swipe at me, and I gasp before I drop a hand to cover his at my hip and push up again. "No, baby. I want it with you. I want you inside me."

"Then have me," he says.

Carefully, I crawl down his lean body until my thighs straddle his hips, and I rise up until I touch the very tip of him to me and sink all the way down. Ryan arches his back, lifting his hips to thrust the last bit inside me, ripping a moan from my chest. He knifes up to a sitting position so we're face-to-face and wraps his arm around me.

I circle my arms around his neck, mindful of the tape at his shoulder, and rise up on my knees to take him again. He fills me up completely like this, and if I don't move, I might die. I work my way up and down his cock, leaning back on my hands, braced on his strong thighs.

His fingers bite into my ass cheek as he leans into me and sucks my nipple deep into his mouth, rolling his tongue over the tip. I drive down onto him as he scrapes his teeth over my flesh and gasp.

"Yes," I pant as I move faster and faster over him while he licks his way over to my other breast. He then drags his tongue up the column of my neck while he pushes his hand up my spine and grabs my hair, making me dip my head so he can take my mouth.

I push against his chest with the flat of my hand as I rock my hips over him, again and again, faster and faster. The climax that was building before is now all-encompassing, and I couldn't stop it if I tried.

I tip my head back, losing his mouth, and cry out as I come. Ryan buries his face in my neck, his body wrapped all around me and deep inside me, and he lets out a roar as he comes.

I hold him tight to me as my breath saws in and out of my lungs. And as it always is with Ryan, he manages to make my entire universe draw down to the one point where we connect, where we're together and we're everything. That is until he takes it all away and turns my nights cold again.

And he always does.

It's like a bucket of ice water is dumped over me. I feel my spine straighten and my muscles tighten. And I know Ryan feels the change in me too.

"Jules?" he asks as he pulls his face from my neck after placing a quick but hot kiss to the center of my throat, but I don't look at him as I climb off his lap and lose his cock.

I race into my bathroom and lock the door. I clean up and then stare at myself in the mirror for far too long, not liking what I see one bit. But I know I have to give Ryan the time he needs to find his clothes as he makes my great escape even in his injured state. Today has been too emotional and eye opening all around. I need a break.

When I've given him plenty of time to leave, I open the bathroom door and walk out into my room, determined not to cry myself to sleep this time, knowing that once again I'll be in my room, all alone.

Only, I'm not.

I stop in my tracks halfway across the room, because Ryan is still lounging on my giant stack of pillows. I have pillows with shams that match my comforter, big euro shams, tons of toss pillows, and a delicate little row pillow, all of which he has stacked up behind his head and shoulders. The covers are tossed aside, and I'm lost in the beauty of his strong, nude form when he's sprawled on my bed. His heavy cock lays soft and glistening against his thigh, and I can't stop staring.

"Don't look at me like that," he warns, but there's humor in his voice.

"Like what?" I ask.

"Like you like the look of my cock."

"I was not—" I start to argue, but he interrupts me, and I feel heat hit my cheeks. I feel heat hit me everywhere, because I'm still naked.

"You were." He laughs. "And I like it. But you can't look at my cock like that right now, baby, because I'm forty-seven not seventeen. I need time to recover and regroup, so I'll let you come cuddle me for a bit, and then I'll fuck you slow."

"Excuse me?"

"Come here, baby," he says, holding his hand out

to me, and I grab it even though I know I shouldn't. "You wore me plum out, and I don't have it in me to watch you get all riled up, not because it's a deterrent, but because I think you're sexy as hell when you do, and as I mentioned before, you wore me out and wrung me dry. I need a minute. So don't make me wanna fuck you right now. Just come and lie down.

His accent is thicker with exhaustion, and I wonder if he intentionally clips it in his everyday life. I have no idea why, because it's very attractive, so I do the only thing I can.

"Okay," I say quietly, and then I climb into bed with him and let him curl me into his side.

And then later on, in the dark dead of night, he rolls me to my back and makes good of his promise to fuck me slow. When we both find completion in each other's arms again, I roll into him voluntarily and fall into a deep, peaceful sleep.

When I wake up the next morning, he's gone, proving I was right all along.

PRESS SECRETARY OFFICIALLY OFF THE MARKET

CHAPTER 8

Apparently, Africa is Out

Taylor Swift's "I Knew You Were Trouble" blares from the speaker on the docking station that sits on top of my nightstand. It's a fitting tribute to the heap of trouble I keep finding myself in over and over again.

And yet, I stay on the merry-go-round.

Without opening my eyes, I blindly reach out and grab my phone from the dock and silence my alarm. I drop it back down on the tabletop before reaching across the bed for the mass of man and muscles I let talk me into bed last night. Again.

And also again, it was a wishful hope I shouldn't have engaged in, because my arms encounter nothing but cool sheets that obviously haven't been slept in for some time.

I open my eyes, and in the early morning light, I can just barely see the indentation in the pillow next to mine, left by his head. I close my eyes tight against the memories of him lounging there, naked and aroused for me, as they slam into my brain. But I can't let that happen.

It's like he was never here, but my body feels otherwise, and the way my leg muscles shake reminds me they were well used the night before.

I see a ton of notifications on my phone, but I don't bother to look at them. I leave it where it's sitting on my bedside table and make my way into the bathroom. I brush my teeth while the water heats up, and I feel my eyes widen as I take in the handprint bruises on my hips. Not once, ever in my entire life, has a lover taken me so roughly or used me up so thoroughly that they left marks on my body. And not once last night did Ryan do anything to hurt me.

I shake off more memories that flash through my brain of the last night we shared together. Something felt… I don't, different, but I can't quite put my finger on it. And trying to is a wasted effort. Nothing on that front will ever change. I need to get my head on straight and end this mess once and for all before someone gets hurt. And by someone, I mean me, because I'm obviously headed for a crash if my behavior yesterday is anything to go by.

I step out of the shower and quickly towel off. I comb out and blow dry my hair and pull it up in a strategically messy ballet bun. I brush my teeth and then dust on more makeup than I honestly feel like having on my face, but I have to be camera ready at any moment. Not to mention a little red lipstick goes a long way toward helping me build back up my armor.

I'm really regretting promising I wouldn't move to Africa last night. I should have jumped on a plane instead of coming upstairs. Now I'm going to have to stick by my decision to stay, and I have a sinking feeling in the pit of my stomach that it was a huge mistake.

I step into my closet and pull on lace panties and a matching bra. I tuck a white poplin blouse into wide-leg gray slacks and wrap a skinny black leather belt around my waist. I thread my diamond studs through my ears and loop my silver watch around my wrist before stepping into a pair of sky-high Louboutins. I grab my cell phone and take the stairs down to the kitchen. I grab my purse and toss my phone inside it before plucking my keys off the hook by the back door and leaving for the day.

I drop my purse on the front passenger seat where it buzzes some more, but I ignore it as I head for my favorite coffee house with a drive-thru. When I pull up to the window with a fake smile on my face and my cash ready to hand over, the kid at the window stutters and makes a weird sound before shaking his head and fixing his expression. That was weird. I wonder what was up with that.

I don't bother to ask. I just get on the highway and head into the capitol. I would find out soon, that was a mistake.

I stay lost in my thoughts as I sip my coffee through the early morning traffic, and again while I park my car and make my way through the security line. I toss my coffee cup in a nearby trashcan and then pass through security, saying a quick good morning to the guards before heading down the hall to my office.

I pull out my cell phone and set it on my desk before dropping my purse into a drawer. There's a stack of papers for my attention in a basket on my desk, and I push out a sigh. Today might be the Mondayest Monday ever. With Ryan's alleged hunting accident, the truth of which the world can never know, and Rachel finally being home—again, something the world can never know about—it's going to be a long press day.

Not to mention House Bill 2250 is still circulating. Jake is probably going to pop a gasket this morning, because I must have heard it mentioned no less than twelve hundred times Saturday night at the State Dinner. That is, when Ryan didn't have me cornered either in a broom closet or after.

I fire up my computer and log in. It's time I get a jump on the day before the morning press conference, when my phone buzzes again, and I reach for it. But before I can look at the screen, my office door swings open with a slam, and Grace's assistant Carter barrels in.

"Where the fuck have you been?" he accuses me, and my stomach clenches. Something must have happened.

"What's happened?" I ask.

"What hasn't happened?" he squawks, pushing a hand through his hair, and I can practically see the tension rolling off him in waves. "How could you be sleeping with the enemy?"

I freeze in my chair. How could anyone know I was with Ryan over the weekend? He's been so careful to sneak in and out without being seen. Hell, I don't even know how or when he gets in. But for Carter to call Ryan "the enemy" doesn't sound right to me.

"So you don't deny it?" he snaps.

"Calm down, Carter," Grace says, panting as she pushes her way into my office. "And Jesus, you're built like a linebacker but move like a jungle cat. It's an unfair advantage in my present state."

"And what state would that be?" he asks, batting his eyelashes innocently.

"Huge," Grace replies on a laugh as she takes a seat in one of the club chairs that face my desk. "Now, what's this about you being in love with my villainous father-in-law?"

"What?" I shout, because I never in my wildest dreams would have thought that's what Carter wanted to confront me about.

"This," he says, tossing the Sunday edition of the Washington paper, "is what everyone is talking about."

I pick up the paper and stare in a horrified fashion at the headlines on the front page. This can't be. Why would he have done this? Why would they? This is so far fucked up I can't even see straight.

"Fuck me," I whisper while I stare at the headlines as if they could jump off the paper they're printed on and bite me.

"Looks like it's all in the family as things heat up between White House Press Secretary and President's Father"

"Why would he say this?" I ask, dumbfounded.

"I don't know," Grace says calmly. "I was hoping you could explain it to me."

"The picture is easy," I start. "Someone must have taken it at the State Dinner, because I was wearing that red dress. But we were never around each other for very long."

"I thought so too," she says thoughtfully. "But why is he giving interviews saying you two are an item?"

"I don't know," I reply and think and think, and then it dawns on me. "Oh God."

"What?" Grace and Carter both ask instantly.

"He approached me," I admit. "About a political alliance, and I politely declined. I would never be overtly rude to the senior senator, but I'm just not interested."

"What happened?" Grace asks.

"He hinted that a political match between us would

be a boon for all involved," I reply.

"I just bet that he did," she mutters.

"I told him I wasn't interested and thought that was it," I answer. "He said he wouldn't wait for me forever, so I figured he'd move on. I think I thought wrong."

"That you did, my dear." Carter sighs. "What a mess."

"I'm not quite sure how to fix this," I admit.

"We'll figure something out," Grace says, and I relax for the first time in a long time. Grace is the best friend I've ever had. "Jake will be happy to know the story is false."

"I bet." I laugh. "Where is Jake anyway? I'm surprised he's not the one breaking down my office door for answers."

"Jake and Rick were called away to some summit meeting or other," she answers. "They should be back tonight."

"Got it." Well, at least I know I can settle some unhappy feelings with my favorite boss and bestie.

"Your parents will be another issue," she says cautiously.

I let out a world-weary sigh. "I know. I don't know what would possess them to give this interview."

Grace watches me carefully, and I hate that she knows me so well, but at the same time, I love that she knows where all of the bodies are buried and still loves me anyway. She really is a great friend.

"You're right. I do know why they gave that interview," I say, amending my previous statement. "They would be over the moon for me to make such a strong match."

"Even if he's old enough to be your grandfather?" Carter asks.

"Even if he's old enough to be my grandfather." I sigh again. "They wouldn't care as long as they got something big out of it."

"But what about love?" Carter is married to a wonderful man who loves him and supports his dream as much as Carter loves him. I'm not sure he can understand a loveless match.

"They don't need trivial things like love to make them happy," I answer quietly.

"Well that's just sad, and we won't stand for it," he rallies. "Now what are we going to do about this?"

A buzzer sounds in my office.

"Shit," I bite out.

"What's that?" Grace asks.

"It's time for a Press Briefing," I answer.

"Oh shit," Carter repeats my earlier curse. "What are you going to do?"

"I'll tell you what I'm *not* doing," I answer him with a grim smile as I push out of my chair. "Apparently, I'm not going to Africa."

"Africa?" he asks as I smooth my palms down the front of my slacks. "What about Africa?"

"Nothing." I smile as I walk out the door.

"Good morning, ladies and gentleman," I say as I step up to the podium in the press room. "I suspect this will be a quick one, as it's a slow news day."

Voices clamor all around me.

"What can you tell us about the hunting accident Captain Black was involved in?" someone shouts.

"Just that there was a minor accident and he is at home recovering," I respond. "He has asked for privacy during his time of healing."

"Has the president changed his stance on HB 2250?" someone else shouts.

"Not to my knowledge. President Chancellor is still openly opposed to House Bill 2250 and its dangerous implications."

"Speaking of the president," someone says, and I mentally brace. "How long have you been romantically involved with the president's father?"

"I am not involved with anyone," I reply with a bored expression pasted on my face. "And if I was, my personal life is not free for public consumption."

"Was the president as happy about the relationship as your parents are?" someone asks.

"I will repeat that I am not romantically involved with anyone at this moment."

"What about yesterday morning's report in the paper?" someone asks.

"What about it?" I reply as if I haven't a care in the

world.

"Both the senior senator and your parents are quoted as being pleased with the match," someone else says. "And you deny it?"

"I don't deny that it seems all parties mentioned would be pleased with a match," I answer and then smile. "I am just not one of those parties. And my parents have not been apprised of my love life for quite some time. As it's my love life and I've previously stated that, one, it's none of your business, and two, there is no love life to speak of, I think you should take my word for it. Now, since that seems all we have for this morning, I will see you all later. Make good choices."

And then I walk out of the room with my head held high.

COULD
WEDDING BELLS
BE RINGING FOR
FLOTUS BFF AND
PRESIDENT'S
FATHER?

CHAPTER 9

Finally something right

Buzz... *Buzz*... *Buzzzzz*...

My phone dances around on the kitchen counter. I had silenced it while I was driving home, because it was ringing nonstop. Worse yet, not only was it ringing nonstop, but it was my mother who was calling.

I'm not ready to deal with my parents and the interview they gave to multiple national news agencies, including my former employers at Eagle News. I know I'm going to have to eventually, but right now, I just can't. What could they have possibly been thinking giving those interviews? And who told them I was involved with anyone, let alone a former U.S. Senator, because I certainly did not.

When I pulled up in front of my house, the whole front was covered with news vans and littered with paparazzi.

This cannot be happening.

I pulled around the house and into my driveway. If they didn't go away soon, I was going to be stuck here for the foreseeable future unless I could find a way to sneak out. Maybe it was time to get a cat. Grace would help me get one… or twelve, because she has a weakness when it comes to rescue felines. But a cat was definitely a valid plan.

Men are nothing but trouble.

"Jules!" one of the reporters shouted. Bobby, I think. We all knew each other in one way or another, because the news circuit is really a very small pool of people. It's weird now that I'm on the other side of the mic. "Is it true?"

"You really want to ask me if all the news you read is true, Bobby?" I asked, and some of the other reporters whispered "Oooohhh" under their breaths. "I think we all know you can't believe everything you read."

"So you're not marrying the senior senator?" someone else asked.

"No," I answered politely. "I'm not currently involved with anyone."

"So why did your family and the senator give those interviews?"

"Now that is the million-dollar question, isn't it?" I asked. "I'll let you know if I find out. Until then, have a good night guys. And let my Uber Eats guy through when he gets here, will ya!"

After that, I made my way into the kitchen, kicking off my heels on my way through the house. I dropped my bag on the marble top of the island and fished out my phone, bringing me to the present.

Seventeen. I have seventeen missed calls from my mother and zero from Ryan. Maybe I should've known. I don't know why I expected him to call me, text me, send up smoke signals or a carrier pigeon or two, something. I don't know.

We're nothing. I know that. But still. I wish he would have reached out. But then again, what would he say to me? *"Thanks for the orgasms. I hope you're happy with your loveless match with a man old enough to be your grandfather."* Because he should know that no one will give me the kind of passion I have with him. And that's the rub, isn't it? There will never be another Ryan Black for me. My heart clutches painfully in my chest. Is this what a broken heart feels like?

I don't know. I don't have the answers, so I grab my phone and order Chinese food. If an order of mu shu chicken and extra cream cheese wontons can't fix it, then nothing can. After I place my order, I make my way upstairs and change out of my slacks and silk blouse and exchange them for something more comfortable but still cute in case the news vans are still on my front lawn when I open the door for the delivery guy. I pull on seafoam-green yoga leggings and a white camisole tank. I top it with an oversized gray sweater that wraps across my front.

I drop my jewelry in the little bowl on my bathroom counter, scrub my face clean, and slather on some moisturizer. I'm home, and they need to know I'm home and not waiting for a man when I open my front door for dinner. I question whether my sweater is too nice or not for home alone activities and if I should toss a sweatshirt on instead. I give up, deciding I can't give it any more of my time to fret over it.

I'm aware that I worry over trivial things when I feel like my life is spinning out of control. And I am spinning out of control. I have a sometimes lover who I can't stay away from, even though I know there is no future there, and I have a man who is publicly claiming I am his lover for no reason that I can figure out, because I have never, not once, ever in my life been his lover. Not to mention he is the father of my boss, who just so happens to be the most powerful man in the world. And add in the fact that the global political climate is heating up uncomfortably, and everything is kind of a mess. I have too many things that need my focus right now, and none of them who are in my bed or wish to be are at the top of the priority list.

I make my way back downstairs and settle in on the sofa. I keep the curtains and blinds drawn, because I am not a Goddamn reality TV show and my life is no one's business. I hear my phone buzz several more times, and I ignore those too.

I pick up the TV remote and turn it on to the old movie channel. My favorite movie *The Women* is just starting. I love the way this mismatched group of women bond together and help each other through tough times. It's kind of like Grace, Angie, and me. We've been friends since that first rush weekend. I don't know how or why, but we just clicked.

Now, Angie is off living her best life with a national football star in a small town in Texas. He gave her a baby after she accidentally became YouTube famous. I should go visit them soon. I need a break to get my head on straight. Although, a little voice in the back of my mind whispers that when Grace went to Texas to get her head on straight, she came back pregnant and engaged to the future president of the United States.

Grace and I stayed in New York until Jake swept her off her feet and offered me a killer gig I couldn't turn down. Somewhere along the way, we added Cara. I wouldn't trade these women for anything in the world. They're more my family than the one I was born into. How crazy is that? Where Grace was raised by loving pacifists with law degrees, I was raised by wolves with grand political aspirations. Not for me, mind you. I'm just supposed to make a strong alliance for my family and breed the next generation. My brother, Gil, however, is being groomed for a political career. But that's neither here nor there.

My rambling thoughts are interrupted by a knock at the door, and I pause the movie. I get up and answer with a smile on my face, taking the delivery kid by surprise. I notice my front lawn is a lot thinner in terms of camped-out news vans, but there are still some there.

"Thanks," I tell him, taking my paper bag full of

deliciousness. I wave to the last of the news crews and head inside.

I shut and lock the door behind me and head into the living room. I drop my bag on the coffee table and then make my way into the kitchen to grab a glass of water. I settle in on the sofa and hit Play on my movie again.

I open the bag and separate my chopsticks before I start building my dinner on a plate. I shovel bite after bite into my mouth and try to watch the movie, but the whole time, I can hear my phone buzzing like a swarm of bees on the stone counter in the next room.

I can't take it anymore, so I set my plate down on the coffee table and make my way into the kitchen. My phone, which had stopped ringing while I walked into the room, starts again. And, also again, it's my mother.

I swipe my finger across the cool glass of the screen and answer, "Hello?"

"Well, it's about time," my mother snaps from across the line. "When I call you, I expect you to answer."

I hate when she talks to me like this. I am thirty-three years old, not five. I have a successful career and have financially supported myself for years. While I have a large trust fund from grandparents who are long since gone from this world, I do not touch it. It sits in the bank. So I have no idea, and I never have, why she would think she could and should speak to me this way. And quite frankly, I don't have the patience for it tonight.

"And I expect you to not give false information to the media about me," I reply. Even I'm impressed with how I keep my tone of voice even and sounding a little unimpressed but not excitable.

She pauses for a minute before she gasps. "How dare you speak to me like that? I'm your mother!"

"And I'm your daughter."

"And you finally did something useful in your life for once," she retorts, and as she does, she sinks the blade of her words deep into my flesh and bone. "I don't know what you did to catch Senator Chancellor's eye, but thank God you finally did something. Your brother, Gil, could use a strong political ally."

"Well, Gil is going to have to keep looking for one," I say quietly. "I won't be able to bridge that gap for him."

"What did you say?" she asks, and her voice is cold as ice.

"I said I won't be able to bridge that gap for Gil. He's going to have to make his own connections."

"I don't care what you have to do to get back in the senator's good graces, but hear me, and hear me now—you are going to fucking do it," she snarls.

"I absolutely will not," I reply. "And you shouldn't ask me to. He's old enough to be my grandfather."

"I don't care if he's old enough to be your great-grandfather," she snaps back, and I wonder when the venom this woman spews at me regularly will stop surprising me. "And I'm not asking. I'm telling. And I'm telling you that if you have to get on your knees and suck a wrinkly old cock that belongs to a man who is old enough to be your grandfather, you damn well will do it to help your brother."

"I think we're done here," I snap.

"We're done when I say we're done, and that's when you agree to do what you're told," she says.

She continues to wax poetic about what a disappointment I am, but I don't listen anymore. I can't. I pull my phone away from my ear and press the red button to end the call. Then I thumb through my contacts and block her number. Then I scroll through and block my dad's numbers as well.

I set my phone down on the kitchen counter and walk back into the living room. I look at my plate and feel what I ate churning in my stomach with the taste of sawdust in my mouth. I have absolutely no appetite anymore. I scoop up the remains of my forgotten meal and walk them to the kitchen trash. I stomp on the little pedal harder than I need to, and the lid flings open. I drop everything in except for my plate, which I walk to the sink.

I turn off the lights, and against my better judgement, I grab my phone from the counter. There are no missed calls since I blocked my parents' numbers. Not even Ryan. Disappointment courses through me. And I scoff at myself in disgust as I take the stairs. What a sad state my life has become: wanting affection from a man who doesn't want me and praise and approval from parents who will give none. I'm a thirty-three-year-old disappointment on all fronts.

Well, not anymore.

I toss my phone on the bed and head into my closet to strip off my sweater. I throw it toward the bench, but it hits the floor, and I do not care one bit about it. I shimmy my leggings down my legs and toss them in the same direction, and then I reach behind my back and unstrap my bra. I pull it through the straps of my camisole and then launch it to the bench.

I walk out of my closet and into the bathroom, brush my teeth, and scrub my face again. I turn out all the lights, pull the covers back, and climb in. I let myself curl up on my side and clutch the blankets just in time for the first sob to bubble up from my chest. One tear after another roll down my cheeks, and I feel from somewhere in the bedding my phone buzz with another incoming call.

"What now?"

I find it in the dark and swipe my finger across the screen. "Hello?"

There's silence, and I wonder if the person hung up, but then Ryan's slow, southern drawl rumbles across the line. "Baby, are you all right?"

Another sob hitches in my chest. And then another.

"Jules? Honey, I need you to answer me."

"No," I whisper my truth. "I'm not okay. But I will

be."

"Jules—" he starts, but I don't let him finish.

"What do you want?" I ask.

"I want to know what the fuck happened today to make you not okay?" Ryan's voice is a brook-no-bullshit tone I'm sure makes other Marines jump into action.

"Nothing." I sigh.

"Jules, the truth. Now."

"It is the truth," I sort of lie. "Today was nothing new."

"So you've always been engaged to a seventy-five-year-old man?" he asks casually after a beat.

"You knew."

"I didn't know you were engaged until this afternoon," he says. "But I knew he was interested in you. He hasn't exactly been keeping it a secret amongst the White House staff."

"Eww. Really?"

He laughs. "I take it the news was mistaken?"

"Don't joke," I snap. "You know I'm not involved with him. Or anyone. I wouldn't have slept with you if I was."

"I had to ask, honey," he says softly.

"No, you didn't," I argue. "You should have just known."

"I didn't—" he starts, but I cut him off again.

"But maybe you should have." I sigh. "Look, Ryan, I'm tired, and I've had a really bad day, and I have to do it all over again tomorrow, so I'm going to let you go so I can try to get some sleep."

"Baby, please," he begs. "I wish you were in my arms."

"But I'm not," I say quietly. "I'm all alone."

And then I hang up. I let my phone drop down to the sheets next to me. I tuck myself back into my protective ball and close my eyes tight while the stinging behind my eyes hits harder than before. And when I can't choke it down, I let the tears come again.

And in the dark, I cry myself to sleep, and just like I told Ryan, I do it all alone.

GLOBAL BILL RE-INTRODUCED TO HOUSE FLOOR

CHAPTER 10

I'm steaming mad. Truth be told, I've been mad since I walked into the offices this morning

A few days later, I rolled out of bed ready to take on the day as I carefully curled my long dark hair to fall in neat waves down my back and dusted a light amount of makeup on my face. Just enough to look good on camera but not so much that I look like I'm trying too hard or unprofessional. I dressed in a red shirt dress with a matching sash belt that ties in a knot. I slipped nude Louboutin heels on my feet and added a slim gold Rolex to my wrist and modest diamond stud earrings. I am who I am, and I will not hide that, but it also doesn't need to be thrown in people's faces either.

I sang along to the radio as I drove to the White House, and I smiled at the Marines who guard the offices as I went through the security protocols to enter. I just had this feeling that it was going to be a great day.

And then I walked into the briefing room.

"HB 2250 is being reintroduced to the house floor this morning," Rick says once everyone is seated around the large conference table. "This time is an even greater donation of power, weapons, and money than before."

"That's insane," someone says, and I can't help but agree. This bill would be handing over a lot of global power the United States has held for ninety years to a country who has done nothing but act against the U.S.

"And this time, it comes with a trillion-dollar reparations check from the U.S.," Rick adds.

"You're kidding. Who would write a bill like that?" I ask.

"That's the trillion-dollar question, isn't it?" Jake prompts softly. "Do we have any leads on where this is coming from?"

"The bill is being introduced by Congressman Grissom this morning, but otherwise, we can't find any ties to him," Rick shares.

"Aren't we still technically involved in a conflict with this nation?" I ask.

"Yes, while it's not a war, per se, we are still involved in a military conflict," Ryan answers, and I nod while not letting my eyes move from his shoulder.

Ryan and I have not spoken more than two words since our odd phone call a few nights ago. I'm pretty sure he realized, like all men do, that I'm more trouble than I'm worth, and that's fine with me. I have enough on my plate right now to add a man to complicate the mix. For most of the week, he was laying low, but now, he's back in the offices.

Lately, there's something different about him. Like he's watching me. And I don't know what to do about it. I cannot acknowledge it, because if I do, I might begin to hope. And I had just begun to hope, when he delivered the kill shot that put the budding affections I held for him recently by making his great escape after I fell asleep. So I can't let the change in him affect me as he watches me. He can; it's a free country, and I can't stop him. But I also don't have to be a willing participant either.

"So our public response should be…?" I ask as I hold my pen just above my notebook, ready to begin crafting my response to any questions that might come up during the press conference later this morning.

"The president's stance on HB 2250 has not changed," Rick said. "And he does not believe that it is in the best interest of the United States and her people."

"Sounds good."

I still had hope by the time the meeting is called that this would be a good day. I was wrong. I hadn't been paying attention when everyone filed out of the briefing room. I was collecting my belongings and lost in my own thoughts about what responses to prep for what questions, so when the door clicked shut a final time, I didn't look up. I thought I was alone, and I thought wrong then too.

"So are you going to talk to me?" Ryan asks. "Or are we back to the silent treatment?"

My head snaps up and I gasp as he moves into the room and closer to me.

"I don't know what you're talking about." That's a lie, I totally do know what he's talking about; I just didn't want to talk about it with him, ever. In fact, I was hoping to never need to talk to Ryan ever again, because every time I do he leaves me bleeding, and I'm not sure I'll survive many more rounds with Captain Ryan Black.

"Sure you do," he says as he presses closer. "You're pissed."

"I'm not," I lie.

"You are," he continues. "I laid it out, and you didn't like it."

"That, we can agree on," I mutter.

"And I realized as soon as I left that you were in a shit mood and being way too harsh," he added.

"Another point for the big man," I mumble, and the skin around his eyes crinkles in the most handsome way.

"But you haven't given me an opportunity to apologize," he finishes.

"Well, consider your apology accepted," I say as I hold my notebook to my chest like a shield. "Now, if you'll excuse me."

"No."

"No, what?"

"You're not excused," he says.

"And you're not my teacher," I snap.

"Baby, there's a lot of things I'd love to teach you," I hear him say.

"Well, forget about them. I don't want to know," I reply. "I think we're done here."

"We're a long way from done, Jules."

I don't wait to hear anything else. I scurry around him and out the door. I'll hide out for as long as I can and get a new phone number. But what I'm not going to do is entertain more opportunities for heartache from Captain Ryan Black.

I make my way to my office and meet with my staff on the press conference scheduled for the noon hour. Grace's office called, but we end up playing telephone tag for a while and never get through before it's time for me to hit the press room.

And I regret ever getting out of bed this morning when I do. But this shit ends now. I am done.

"Good morning," I greet the associate press as I take the podium. "We'll make it a quick one this morning, as there is much to do."

Hands go up and voices clamor all around the room. One voice rings out above the rest. "Why is the president against a bill that could help our country?"

And then another voice shouts, "What are his ulterior motives?"

"Let me stop you all right there," I say, holding up my hands, palms out. "Let me ask you a few questions. Please raise your hand if the answer is yes. Have any of you read the original House Bill 2250 that the president vetoed several weeks ago? No? Well I have in all of its four hundred and seventy-nine page glory. Have any of you read the updated version that was introduced to the house floor this morning by Congressman Grissom? No again? Well, I have, as my staff and I just spent the bulk of today combing through it, and I can tell you if House Bill 2250 was frightening before, it's now *terrifying*, as its sole purpose seems to be to give money, weapons, and power to a nation and its friends who have done nothing but perpetrate violence and acts of terror against the United States and her people. This is not the goodwill gesture you have been sold. I can also assure you the president takes this very seriously, and he and his staff are doing all they can to make sure the American people are safe and protected. So I suggest you all do your homework before you come to me with more asinine questions like these, and next time we meet, please be prepared. Thank you and good day."

And then I walked out of the press room with the snaps and pops of cameras and the shouts of the associate press trying to get my attention, but they've had all they're going to get from me today. There is a long weekend this weekend, and we are headed to Vegas for Cara and Rick's wedding "part deux," as Carter and Grace like to call it. I am ready to take on the weekend and have a little bit of fun.

What I don't know now, but I would find out later, is that little bit of fun could cost me everything if I'm not careful.

But then again, some lessons have to be learned the hard way.

SECOND CHANCE ROMANCE? WHITE HOUSE CHIEF OF STAFF SPOTTED WITH ESTRANGED EX-WIFE.

Las Vegas, Nevada

I'm a little tipsy.

Okay, I'm more than a little tipsy. I'm drunk.

Last week, when Rick told Jake that he was marrying Cara this weekend, Jake told Grace, because that's apparently what married people do. And then Grace told me, as besties do. And then Grace, Carter, and I planned the Vegas wedding of a lifetime. The theme is Classic Vegas. I had no idea what that was, having been raised on the Upper East Side, but I know class.

The three of us planned every detail.

When Rachel said she wanted pink dresses for her and her mom, we found the most gorgeous rose-gold beaded dress. It's not the typical wedding dress, but then again, this isn't your typical wedding. And we topped it with a leather jacket for after that has a rock-and-roll design Cara hand-painted on the back. It's totally fitting for a fashion stylist to wear after her wedding.

It's going to be soft candles, music, champagne, and all the people Rick and Cara are close to. And we have a surprise for them. When Rick told us they were married by an Elvis impersonator years ago, we decided that with all the class and style we were giving them, we'd also give them a little Vegas flair and a walk down memory lane at the same time.

We flew in yesterday and hit the ground running to our luxury suites at the Paris Hotel and Casino. Jake couldn't come with us for obvious reasons. He flew in only an hour ago with his entourage, which is really the groom's entourage. We brought Cara and Rachel with us. Rachel was having the time of her life with Gus down in the arcade while we made sure all our plans were in place. And they were.

I can't wait to see her walk down the aisle in it tomorrow. It's going to be perfect.

Now we're all in a private room for VIPs in the best steakhouse in Vegas. It's off the strip and a local hotspot, so you know it's fantastic. I enjoyed a perfect dinner complete with four vodka martinis with blue cheese olives and great company. I forgot how much I missed our regular girls' nights with Grace.

"This has been so much fun," I say after Grace tells another tall tale from our days at NYU.

"I forgot how much I missed our regular LBD dinners," Grace replies.

"LBD?" Ryan asks.

"Little Black Dress," Grace answers. "We used to get dressed up and go out to dinner and catch up every other Saturday."

"Life got intense," I insert, shrugging off the feeling that life is passing me by. But tonight is not about me, and I'm not going to let it be either. "Speaking of intense. The town car should be here in twenty minutes to take you to the courthouse for your marriage license. You have all the documents, right?"

"Yes," Cara says, but Rick interrupts her, looking a little sheepish.

"We won't be needing them."

I swear to God you can hear a pin drop. Cara's face goes pale, and I can see she's thinking what we all thought, which is crazy. Rick won't leave her at the altar, will he? I never would have thought he'd be the kind of guy to do it; then again, I never thought he'd be the kind of guy to have a secret wife and daughter either.

I look around the table and see shocked faces on everyone. That is on everyone except Jake, who is smiling like a lunatic.

"Why won't we need our documents to get a marriage license?" Cara asks quietly.

"Because we won't be getting a marriage license,"

he answers with a stupid smile on his face and a wild look in his eyes.

"Why not?" she murmurs calmly.

"Because we don't need one."

"Now, excuse me—" Grace wades in, going all mama bear for our girl.

"That's right—" I add, but Rick cuts us both off.

"We don't need one, because we're already married." He drops that bomb on the table.

"Honey," Cara says, clearly thinking her intended is drunker than he seems. "I signed divorce papers before they were served to you."

"I know," he says, still smiling like an idiot.

"So we're divorced. And getting married in the morning."

"We're having a wedding," he replies cryptically, making Jake burst out laughing. He's clearly in on the inside information.

"What's going on here?" Grace turns her accusations on her husband, who holds his hands up in surrender and smiles as he shakes his head.

"So, funny story," Rick says. "When I got home and had the divorce papers waiting for me, I was so mad."

"I know, honey," Cara says gently. "And I am so sorry."

"I know." He smiles at her and places a quick kiss

on her mouth. "But that's not the funny part."

"Well then, get to it, man!" Grace shouts, clearly losing her patience.

"I looked at those papers, and I just got so fucking mad," he says by way of an explanation. "And then I got rip-roaring drunk. So drunk that I lit them on fire in the kitchen sink and set off the smoke detector in the old apartment."

"What?" Cara asks with wide eyes.

"So I didn't sign them or file them," he says. "Because I couldn't, and I didn't want to."

"What does that mean?" she asks, and he answers her immediately.

"That we've been married this whole time."

And with that, I throw my head back and laugh.

"I'm just going to go call the car service," Carter says before standing from the table.

"I'll go with you and call the courthouse to cancel their reservation," his husband Todd says.

I have a smile on my face, because all is right in the world of my people. I would do anything for this crazy group, Cara and Grace in particular. I toss back the last of my martini and pick up the little skewer of olives and use my teeth to pluck one from the stick.

"Now it's Jules's turn," Grace says with a knowing look on her face.

"Jules's turn for what?" Jake asks innocently, and I could kill him.

"To find a man and settle down," she answers, and I choke on my olive. Ryan slaps me hard on the back while laughing. I have no earthly idea what he could find so funny about this situation.

"Enough meddling, wife," Jake says as he stands and holds out a hand to Grace, which she takes.

We've already squared away the bill in advance, so everyone is free to leave. Gus and the guys are off duty this weekend and decide to take in the sights before tomorrow's festivities, so they head out. Their stand-ins quietly follow Grace and Jake out of the building after they've said their goodnights. And then before I know it, it's just Ryan and me.

"I'll see you back to the hotel," he says quietly, but it's in a tone that leaves no room for argument.

"You don't have to do that," I hurry to say. "I'll be all right."

He just repeats his earlier statement. "I'll see you back to the hotel."

"Okay."

Ryan holds his hand out to me, much the same way Jake did for Grace, and I take it. He pulls me up from my seat, and he picks up my black pashmina, holding me to face him, our bodies close together as he wraps it around my shoulders. The move is so intimate that I find myself a little self-conscious. I don't look at his eyes but instead stare intently at the space of tan skin at the base of his throat that's exposed by the buttons of his dress shirt undone at the collar.

He makes an amused sound from deep in his chest, and I look up in time to see his sexy mouth twitch. I'm not sure what's so amusing, but even so, I'm surer that I don't want to know what he finds so funny, so I clutch the ends of my wrap together at my chest and reach for my beaded black clutch.

"Ready?" he asks, and I can hear his smile in his voice.

"Yes," I mumble. "Thank you."

And then Ryan leads me through the restaurant and out the side door to a waiting town car. The driver opens the rear door, and I slide in with Ryan following behind me. Once the driver closes the door, I realize Ryan has moved so close, not giving me space on the bench seat, so I scoot to the door. I get about a half an inch away before his firm hand grips my thigh to stop my movement and then, to my shock, hauls me right back.

I gasp at his highhanded move, but Ryan says nothing. He also doesn't move his hand for the entire ride. And what should have been like a bucket of cold water over my head, coupled with the copious amounts of vodka in the martinis I drank with dinner, it only serves to turn me on more.

The car stops at the secret side entrance to the Paris Hotel, because we're still trying to keep a low profile. The driver pulls the door open, and Ryan slides out before turning to offer me a hand to help me from the car.

"Thank you," I say quietly, my hand still held tightly in his. I think he'll let go of me and be on his way. We haven't spoken much—not more than a few words here and there—since he cornered me after the meeting, so it surprises me when he doesn't immediately let me go. Instead, he looks into my eyes, and whatever he sees there seems to make him come to some kind of resolution. What, I do not know.

What I do know is the look he's giving me sends a tingle shimmying up my spine.

But it also scares the shit out of me.

"I'll see you to your room," he finally says.

"That's all right," I reply quietly as I try to extract my hand from his. "I'll be okay."

"I'll see you to your room," he repeats as he did at dinner, and there is a determined look rolling across his handsome face, so I relent.

"Fine."

And with my hand in his, Ryan walks me through the casino and to the elevator bank, where we ride the car to the twenty-eighth floor. He watches me with an intent look on his face I can't decipher.

When the elevator doors glide open, he follows me down the hall to my suite. I pop open my clutch and fish out my room key. My heart races in my chest, and it's so loud I think that maybe Ryan can hear it too as he stands right behind me, the heat from his body scratching my back.

He plucks the key from my hand, deftly unlocks my

door, and pushes it open for me. I step into the room, and he follows me in, letting the door click closed behind us. I toss my bag onto the coffee table in the sitting room. My hands shake just a little as I take off my jewelry.

Ryan slips his dark suit coat down his arms and tosses it over the back of the sofa before he slowly stalks toward me, step by step, herding me like a sheep dog toward the bedroom.

"Ryan—" I start, but he just keeps prowling toward me, one step at a time.

"I want you," he says. "And I know you want me too."

I gasp. Not only because of the way he's speaking to me, the audacity and the arrogance, but also because he's right. I fear there will never be a time I don't want Ryan Back as badly as I do.

"Do you?" he asks softly. "Want me?"

"Yes," I whisper.

"Then take off your dress," he orders as he reaches to his wrist and unbuttons his cuffs.

I reach for the buckle on my wide belt and unclip it, letting it fall to the floor. My dress is made of hundreds of folds and pleats of black tulle cinched at my waist so that it looks like a big ruffle at the top and bottom, giving the illusion that one might get a peek of flesh if I lean the wrong way. They won't; the inside is fitted and lined, and it zips up the back, but the illusion is sexy as hell.

I watch as he slowly unbuttons each button of his shirt and shrugs it down his shoulders. He reaches for the buckle of his leather belt, and it clanks as he opens his suit pants and lets them fall to the floor. He steps out of them and his shoes and stands before me in nothing but a pair of dark-gray boxer briefs, and the outline of his full cock makes me clench my thighs together.

Ryan sees my move and smirks, and I hurry to reach behind me and pull down the zipper of my dress. The material parts, and I let it fall to the floor.

"On the bed," he says, his voice rough. "Now."

I kick off my heels and hurry to lie down on the center of the bed. Ryan climbs onto the bed from the foot and peels my panties down my legs. I allow them to fall open for him, and he circles my opening with his fingers.

And then finally, he drives them deep inside me.

"Ohhh… yes. Yes!" I chant as he thrusts two fingers into my pussy. My hips arch up to meet him. "Please!" I beg him for more.

"Mmm." He chuckles, low and throaty, because he's enjoying teasing me, keeping me on the edge. Ryan is playing with me tonight, toying with me to drive my passion high and higher.

"Please!" I need him so badly.

I have never wanted anyone or needed anyone the way that I need Ryan Black. If someone had told me, back in New York, that I would become addicted to the body of a man and the way that he uses it to bring me pleasure, a man that I'm not always sure that I like or he likes me, I would have laughed in their face. But it's true. I don't just need him, *I'm addicted to him*. And I have a sinking suspicion that I will never be the same again after being at the sexual mercy of Ryan Black.

Ryan pushes his underwear down and grips his thick, veiny cock in his fist before rubbing the flushed tip through my wetness then up to stroke my clit, making me bite my lip to keep from crying out, because my torture only seems egg him on.

"Ahhh," I moan as he finally notches the very tip of him at my center and slides in all the way.

The muscles in his thighs and ass flex and ripple as he pulls out to the tip only to thrust back in, making my tits bounce like a porn star. He grips my hips so tight in his hands that I know will leave marks on my body, and I don't care one bit.

He pumps into me over and over again. My hands grip the sheets of the bed tight as I arch my back while he fucks me into oblivion. No one has ever been as good as Ryan, and I feel deep in my soul that no one ever will.

My jaw drops down on a silent scream, and my eyes close as I find completion in his arms. Ryan drives deep once, twice, before he plants himself deep as he comes.

It wouldn't be until much later that I realize he never held me close, he never let us touch skin-to-skin, and how much I would miss it. Instead, I curl up into the covers and fall asleep thinking Ryan would join me when he came back from the bathroom. Instead, he never does.

I shouldn't be surprised really. My life is nothing but empty promises and disappointment.

RUMORS CIRCLE
THAT A CERTAIN
PRESS SECRETARY
AND FORMER
SENATOR SPENT THE
WEEKEND HOLED UP
IN ROMANTIC CABIN

CHAPTER 12

Rumor Has It

Washington D.C.

"Jules! Jules!" a reporter I know shouts when I walk out of my house this morning.

Not this again.

I was hoping that after a long weekend away, they would have finally given up their post on my front lawn. It was wishful thinking. Soon, the world will catch wind of Cara and Rick retying the knot, and as awful as it sounds, I hope the press gives them a little love for a while. We could all use a feel-good story right now. Anything to get the nation's minds off HB 2250 and why people would back something as crazy as that.

"Jules! Rumor has it you spent a romantic weekend with a certain former senator," someone else calls out.

"Guys," I say, rolling my eyes. "Really?"

"What?" my ex asks from off to the side, drawing my attention to him. "America wants to know."

"Gunner!" I say with a genuine smile for a friend. "What are you doing here?"

I walk right up to the man who was once my lover and wrap my arms around him. He picks me up off the ground and swings me around. We were close when we were dating, and while we drifted apart after we broke up because there was someone new for him to share that closeness with, I still hold no hard feelings. I care for Gunner and want him to be happy. I want him to be who he is and be free to do that. There are no hard feelings on my end and there never were.

"Your impending nuptials to the president's father has the network's bigwigs drooling," he says, and the smile falls right off my face.

"Et tu, Gunner?" I reply, letting him see my frustration play out on my face. "Not you too."

"We all have to eat." He shrugs. "So how about an exclusive for an old friend?"

I shoot him my sternest glare. "The exclusive is that there is no exclusive," I say loud enough for everyone to hear me. "Come on, you all know how busy our careers are. I have literally no time to be involved with anyone."

"Sure, Jules," Gunner says. "But if I find out you're lying…." He lets the words hang in the air, and a shiver wracks up my spine, because I wasn't completely truthful. Then again, how could he know I've spent a few evenings with the president's aide-de-camp?

I smile brightly. "There's nothing to find out, guys. Now, I do hope you're all prepared for this week's briefing on House Bill 2250."

After a jaunty wave to the rest of the news crews in front of my house, I beep the locks open on my car and jump in. I pull through my favorite coffee place on my way to work and have just about finished my favorite skinny vanilla latte, a splurge for me, when I pull into the staff lot.

I make my way through security and into my office. I'm keeping my mental fingers crossed for a slow news day, but even I know that's wishful thinking. I haven't heard from my parents yet—although they're still blocked on my cell phone, but they have their ways.

I fire up my computer and see I have an email from my brother, Gil.

Hey, sis.

I'll be in town on business this week. Want to catch dinner with your big brother? Also, Mom's been asking about you. Do your favorite brother a favor and call her to get her off my back if nothing else.

Love you, sis,

G

    Frustration pours through me and I feel something ugly slither in my belly and it's not nice. My whole life, Gil has been the golden child and I've been the red headed stepchild. Gil has never once received the sharp end of her tongue. He's never been told to watch his weight or to not bother with an education because someday he would make a pretty bride in the society pages. He's also never held our father's disappointment. That mantle is solely my own to wear. So the fact that he's asking me to get mom off of his back does not endear his cause to me, whether he's joking or not.

Hey, Gil,

Yes to dinner. No to calling Mom. You're just going to have to suck it up, buttercup. I'm not bending to her wishes this time. She's yours now.

Love,

Your favorite sister

I don't think about it once I've typed out my response, and I hit Send before I can doubt myself. Gil has always been a great big brother and my friend growing up, even though he's so much older than I am. He's always looked after me, even if he never protected me from our parents. Actually, he's the same age as Ryan when I stop to think about it.

The phone on my desk rings.

"Hello?" I answer.

"Ms. Fairchild, the president would like to see you in the Oval in ten minutes," the secretary on the other end of the line says without greeting. She's kind of a bitch. I know that's not nice of me to say, but I think she has a thing for Ryan. Well, good for her. She can have him. I'm done with men.

"I'll be there," I reply, and as soon as the words are out of my mouth, I hear the line disconnect and hold the receiver out in front of me like it's a poisonous viper. "Good talking to you too. Thanks for the gab."

"Talking to yourself?" Ryan asks from my doorway, making me jump.

"Eek!"

He lets out a delectable chuckle. "Babe, what are you doing?"

"Shh!" I snap.

"What?" Ryan asks, and I can hear amusement in his tone.

"Don't 'what' me!" I whisper-yell. "And don't call me babe either."

"Why not?" he asks with a smile on his face. "You like it when I call you babe."

"I like it in certain scenarios," I admit. "But not here. Someone might hear you."

"You like it."

"I don't."

"You do," he says, stalking his way into my office. "You like it when I'm fucking you. And you like it now."

"Don't be crass."

"You like that too," he purrs, and dammit he's right, but I won't admit that to him or anyone.

"I don't have time for this," I say. "I have a meeting in the Oval in five minutes and just enough time to get there."

"What a coincidence," he says with a smile. "So do I."

"Of course you do," I mutter under my breath, but Ryan clearly hears it, because his smile grows even wider.

"Shall we?" he asks, holding the door open for me.

"Thank you," I reply even though I don't want to, because good manners were practically beaten into me at an early age. It doesn't bode well to have a society wife who is rude and common at dinner parties.

We walk side by side down the hallway of the staff offices and through to the Oval Office. The bitchy secretary gives Ryan her best come-hither look, and it takes about everything in me not to roll my eyes.

"I saw that," he says under his breath.

"Saw what?" I ask innocently.

"Don't be like that," he says. "It's unbecoming."

I bite down on my bottom lip to keep from screaming at him. If there is one person on the planet who could make me crazier than Ryan Black, I don't want to know them. I'm surprised my hair doesn't completely stand on end every time I'm around him.

"The president will see you now," one of the Marines guarding the door says.

They pull open the doors, and Ryan and I step into the Oval Office, and I take it all in. It's been months that we've been working here and Jake and Grace have been living in the residence, and I'm still not used to it. The history, the architecture, and the beauty of it all still take my breath away.

"Good to see you both," Jake says when the doors shut behind us. "Come on in and let's get down to business."

"What's going on?" I ask as I sit down on one of the sofas. Jake sits across from me and crosses his ankle over his opposite knee in that casual way men do. Ryan stands beside me but leans a hip against the arm of the sofa. It's a casual but ready stance.

"What I want to know is why my father is giving sit-down interviews with Brenda Watson on uniting our families," Jake prompts, and I feel like all the air has been sucked out of my lungs. And not only has all of the air been sucked out of my lungs, it's been sucked out of the room. And Ryan, who was casual, is now anything but.

"Brenda Watson?" I ask in a small voice. "Brenda Watson of the big cable network emotional celebrity sit-down interviews where everyone always cries?"

"That's the one," he answers.

"Fuck," Ryan bites out.

"I don't know," I answer honestly. I've never even been on a date with him.

"Well that's interesting, because he seems to be under the impression that you're engaged," Jake adds, not helpfully at all, because Ryan is obviously—to me, anyways—negative two seconds away from completely losing his mind and ripping the room apart like a barbarian.

"Are you shitting me?" he asks Jake in a low voice.

"Why would he do that?" I ask. "I don't understand."

"Has he ever given you the impression that he was romantically interested in you?" Jake asks.

"No," I reply and then change my answer almost immediately. "Yes. As we were lining up to enter the State Dinner, he told me that we would make a strong political match, and I politely turned him down. He implied you would look favorably on uniting our families."

"I bet he did," Jake growls. "I do not like the idea of marriages made for political or financial gain. He was pushing me toward one when I finally caught Grace's eye."

"Sure, that's what we'll call it," I snark with a sweet smile on my face, and Ryan laughs. It's not public knowledge, but those in the inner circle know Jake and Rick had staged a blackmail setup in order to force Grace into a public relationship with Jake. My friend thought it was fake, but in the end, it was all real. Swoon.

"True," Jake says with a smirk. "But that doesn't explain your parents' interview over the weekend."

"Actually," I say, holding up my hand like I'm in school again, "I can answer that one too."

"I'm all ears."

A phone on the desk rings, and Jake stands, making his way back to the desk. He picks up the receiver and speaks, "Hello? Just a second."

He presses a button on the phone and sets the receiver back in the cradle.

"Hey, Rhys," Jake says to the room. "I'm here with Jules and Black."

There was a pregnant pause, and then the deepest voice spoken in a heavy brogue I've ever heard speaks.

It's not quite Scottish, so I can't place it. "Am I free to speak here?"

"Yes," Jake answers. "You're protected."

I don't have a chance to dive into that one too deeply before the conversation takes off, but I have so many questions. My Spidey senses are tingling.

"I hear congratulations are in order," Rhys says, and I watch Jake bite his lip to keep from laughing.

I roll my eyes.

"We were just trying to get to the bottom of that," Jake says.

"I figured it wasn't as it seems," he tells us, and I think for a second I would be happy to listen to him read the phone book or the dictionary his voice is so damn pretty.

"I take it there's a reason you called," Jake urges.

"There are things in play that you don't understand."

"No," Jake says, the fun tone of the room becoming serious.

"I found her," he replies quietly.

"So it's true?"

"It's true," Rhys confirms.

"Be safe," Jake says.

"You as well, mate." And then the line goes dead.

"What was that?" I ask.

"I think your question is more a 'who was that?'" Ryan corrects.

"Okay," I amend. "Who was that?"

"That was George Rhys John Aidan Alexander," Jake answers. "Crowned Prince of the Isle of Saints."

"Holy shit," I breathe.

"He has some stuff going down, so you can't speak of this conversation," he warns.

"I won't."

"This is serious, Jules," Ryan adds. "No one can know."

"Okay, I get it." And I do. I have enough crazy shit going on in my life; I don't need to know what a crowned prince has going down that would put that shocked tone in Jake's voice. In fact, I don't want to know anything else. I need those *Men in Black* guys to come erase my memory. Actually, that sounds great, because then I could also forget Ryan's beautiful cock and the magnificent orgasms he gives me with it, his hands, and his mouth.

"Now, back to your parents," he says, pulling me out of my thoughts, and I let out a sigh.

"They want nothing more than for me to make a strong match for them," I explain. "My whole life, I was raised with the knowledge that I was expected to become the wife of a powerful businessman who could benefit my father, or a strong politician who could help my brother with his political aspirations."

"How is Gil?" Jake asks.

"Wanting me to call my mother so she will leave him alone," I answer.

"And how's that working out for him?"

"Not so good," I reply and watch his lips twitch as he tries not to laugh. It must be difficult to be the president of the United States and have to try and be dignified all the time. "I fear my parents must have caught wind of the senior senator's interviews and jumped on the bandwagon. I've since set them straight."

"And what did they say to that?" Ryan asks from beside me.

"That I'm a disappointment, because what better link for Gil than to have his sister be the stepmother to the current president," I answer. "We're not currently speaking."

"Good girl," he murmurs for my ears only.

"I've told the press repeatedly that I'm not currently involved with anyone."

"We'll see about that," Ryan mutters again.

"I think they'll get the hint and give up on it… *eventually.*"

"Let's hope so," Jake says. "For now, I think you should lie low for a few days. Come back Thursday, and we'll see where we're at."

"Okay," I say quietly. I can't help but feel like I'm a disappointment. If I were better at my job, I wouldn't be in this pickle to begin with.

"It'll all be okay, Jules," Jake says, and I just nod and stand up, but I'm not so sure if I agree with him.

I walk out of the Oval Office and back through the halls to my own little office. I shut down my computer and grab my bag. I make my way through the building, climb into my car, and head home. Fortunately, when I get there, my street is empty. I pull my car into the garage and lock it up so no one can tell whether I'm home or not.

And then I go inside to try to figure out where I went wrong in my life. Also unfortunately, I have no answers.

The feel of the sheets slithering down my body wakes me from a sleep that was less than restful, and I know instantly that I'm not alone.

Ryan cups the back of my head as I turn from my belly to my side and presses his mouth to mine. I gasp against the hard pressure of his lips, and he licks inside my mouth. He rolls me to my back and whisks the tank I wore to bed up and over my head before he licks at the seam of my lips again, and again I let him inside.

I'd like to say it's because I was asleep, that I was drowsy and didn't know what I was doing, but the second Ryan touches me, he and I both know I want nothing else but him inside me. I wrap my arms around his shoulders and try to pull him toward me. I want him to hurry, I need him so much, but he won't give in.

He lets me go, and I flop to my back on the bed. I watch as he does that sexy thing men do when they reach behind their shoulders and grab their tee with one hand and haul it over their heads. I stare at the muscles of his chest and shoulders flex and his firm belly, and I lick my lips as I watch him trail his hands down his abs to the fly of his jeans and pull, popping open half the buttons at once. I have to roll my bottom lip into my mouth to keep from moaning out loud when he tucks his fingers into the waistband and pushes both his jeans and his underwear to the floor, letting his long, hard cock spring free and bob below his navel.

And then he climbs to the foot of the bed between my legs, grabs the cotton sleep shorts I'm wearing and my panties, and tears them down my legs. With his hands to my inner thighs, Ryan firmly pushes my legs to fall open, exposing me to him, and the look in his eyes when he looks at all of me sets me on fire.

He wraps his fist around the base of his erection and grips it tight before stroking himself once… and then twice… all while he looks at me. There's something highly erotic about your lover touching themselves while they're with you.

"I think tonight I wanna watch you," he says, and his slow, southern drawl is deepened by lust.

"W-w-what?" I stammer as all the oxygen rushes

out of my lungs.

"Touch yourself," he commands as he trails a fingertip from my clavicle to my breast and down around my nipple, making it bud under his attention. His eyes watch as he swirls the digit in question around and around and then snap up to lock on mine. "I want to see how you touch yourself, and then I want to watch you make yourself come while my cock is deep inside you."

I don't know why I do it. I shouldn't do it. I shouldn't want to do it. But his words have me so hot and bothered. He's so turned on wanting to watch me that *I'm* turned on. He sits back on his heels when I place my palm on my belly and slowly move it down, down, down, until it's between my thighs and I can feel my own wetness.

I trace my opening with a fingertip and watch his heavy lids lower as he watches me. My breath catches when I brush my clit, and he bites his lip and strokes his cock in his fist. I could watch him like this all day.

I press my finger inside me and pump twice before I circle my clit over and over. My legs press farther open, and I rock my hips into my hand.

I tip my head back and close my eyes as the tension radiating out from my center travels up through my body, and I know I'm close.

"Look at me," Ryan says, and his voice is rough with need—his need for me—and my eyes instantly pop open. "Look at me when you take yourself there."

"Yes," I whisper.

And then he's there. I feel the very tip of him press into me. He grips my thighs in his hands and leans forward as he drives into me.

I can feel where he and I join as he brushes against my fingers, and I revel in it. I come alive under his touch.

"Don't stop," he growls as he drives deep only to slowly slide out and drive back in, over and over. "Make yourself come."

I had stopped to just feel. To feel where our bodies come together. To feel how he overwhelms me in the best of ways.

But now it's time to move.

I stroke my clit again, circling my fingers around and around while Ryan plunges faster and faster.

He pins me to the mattress by my thighs, holding me open so he can pump in and out of me again and again. He moves faster and faster as I move my hand, driving us both closer and closer to the edge.

"Give it to me," he growls. "It has to be now."

And I know he's walking the knife's edge just as I am, and knowing I've brought him there, that I do that to him, throws me off the cliff.

"Ryan," I whisper, and then I tip my head back and come.

"Yes," he groans as he drives deeper, harder, faster again and again, and then his fingers tighten almost painfully on my thighs as he plants himself deep one more time and follows me over the edge, taking me with him yet again.

I lie there with my eyes closed for who knows how long. He sits there on his knees, touching me everywhere. He skates his hands down my legs and up my arms, just touching me wherever he can with no pattern at all.

My eyes pop open when he gently brushes a lock of my hair back from my face and then brushes the backs of his fingers down my temple.

"You're so fucking beautiful."

I don't know what to say to that, so I don't say anything at all. He watches me for a minute as if I should say or do something, even though I don't know what, and then he pulls out and curls to his side. He pulls my back to his front and settles the blanket over us.

I think he might be settling in to stay, and I let all the muscles in my body relax one by one, and I let out a deep breath.

It's then he rolls me to my back and makes love to me. It's slow and it's sweet and it's tender. So much so that it brings tears to my eyes. There's so much emotion welling up inside me, and I realize I have feelings for Ryan. That somewhere along the way, he wormed his way into my heart, and I think maybe I wasn't wrong for letting him in my bed all this time.

And then when it's over, he places one last kiss to my lips and pulls out. And keeps on rolling out of the bed. I watch in horror, like one might watch a terrible car wreck on the interstate, as he steps into his underwear and jeans and then pulls his shirt over his head. He steps into a pair of Sperry's, and then he's gone without a backward glance.

Too bad the jerk stepped on my heart on his way to the door.

FUNERAL OF LATE SOCIALITE WAS WHO'S WHO OF POLITICS

CHAPTER 13

"In the sweat of thy face shalt thou eat bread, till thou return unto the ground; for out of it wast thou taken: for dust thou art, and unto dust shalt thou return," the Pastor reads from his Bible.

It's an unseasonably cold spring day as we stand in the crowd of mourners as Ashley Jeffries, New York socialite, former girlfriend of the President of the United States, and all-around rotten bitch from hell is laid to rest.

I know we shouldn't speak ill of the dead, but I'm also not entirely sure she hadn't risen from hell instead of being born from her mother like other mammals.

Really, I would be more considerate if she deserved it at all. Instead, she perpetrated one heinous act against my friends after another.

"Can you believe it?" someone whispers to another. "A car accident?"

"More like a Car*a* accident," I mumble under my breath to Grace, who has to bite her lip to keep from laughing. It wouldn't do at all for the First Lady of the United States to be caught laughing at the graveside service of her husband's former lover. Even if the comment is more than accurate. After all, she did try to kill my Cara after she kidnapped her daughter. Not to mention, she shot Ryan. And in an effort to escape, Cara hit her in the head with a metal folding chair, breaking her neck.

But that's need-to-know information. Somehow, the Jeffries family spun her death as a tragic car accident instead of justifiable homicide. No one is sure how that happened. And we've been looking into it.

By all accounts, Ashley Jeffries was nothing more than an empty-headed socialite intent on marrying into the highest echelon of political power and causing hate and discontent, no doubt. I've known her for years. We grew up in the same social circles, after all. In fact, I would swear she was just the kind of woman my parents would be hellbent on marrying to my brother, Gil.

Hell, they wanted nothing more than for me to be Ashley Jeffries, other than the dead as a doornail part. Although, maybe that part too. I'm useless, after all, and I have a portion of the family trust they can't have, because I've already reached the payout terms.

I'm sure they would've finally found some value in me if I had set my cap for Jake like Ashley had. Sure,

Jake is hot, everyone has always known that, but there was something about how much my longtime bestie hated him. As it would turn out, Grace protested too much. She was awfully vociferous in her complaints about Jake, not because she hated him, but because she was attracted to him. And it all seemed to work out in the end. They're happily married and expecting a baby this summer. Well… I mean, it all worked out for everyone but Ashley, who got herself dead. But I digress.

Her dad looks this way, and for a second, he looks… angry. There's a level of malice that crosses his face that I have never seen before. And I grew up in a home with Gilbert and Alexandra Fairchild as my parents. The level of anger they are capable of would be shocking to anyone else, and it was everyday fair in our not so happy home.

So to see such anger, such hatred on Mark Jeffries's face is alarming. And it's directed at me. I've known Mark for years. He's an acquaintance of my own dad, and he has always been very cordial to me. I mean, it's not like I clobbered his daughter with a card chair. Although I would have in the same situation. And as I mentioned, she did shoot Ryan. So to see him so angry with me is alarming. And then it's just… gone, like it was never there at all. How odd.

They lower the casket into the ground, and I watch as mourners throw sand or flowers into her grave. And then out the corner of my eye, I see a man approach Ryan, who is standing just a few people in our entourage over from me. I pretend not to see him.

He says in a low voice, "I'm just the messenger."

He hands Ryan a small note, and then he walks away.

The hair on the back of my neck stands on end. We never heard anything more about Rachel's kidnapping, but then again, we all thought Ashley was just a pawn and we always had. But what if it wasn't that simple? I look back at Mark and see him watching Jake now. It makes me uncomfortable. And then he heads to the waiting limo, and I watch as he leaves.

The service is over. Thank God.

"We need to meet," Jake says low as our group gathers for a word while the service breaks up. "The residence will do."

"Willco," Ryan says before we all depart on nods to meet at the White House residence.

I depart from the group, climb in my car, and head back toward the capitol after watching Gus herd Jake and Grace into their vehicle. Ryan gets in with them, as does Rick.

Cara is missing from our little funeral party, because she thought it was tacky to attend the funeral service of the person you accidentally killed in self-defense. She's clearly not in politics… or the media for another thing. She's not ruthless enough. My colleagues would take me out and dance at my funeral if it meant they got my job.

God, I love my job.

As I watch them all depart, it reminds me that I'm on the outside looking in. I belong, but I don't. I wonder if I should attend the meeting at the residence or if I'm not important enough, when my phone sounds with a text alert.

RYAN: In case you're wondering, Jake means you too.

ME: I wasn't.

RYAN: You were.

ME: Was not. And also, you don't know that he means me too. I'm not really involved in this.

RYAN: You're involved.

ME: You don't know that!

JAKE: Come to the meeting. You two are giving me gray hair.

Well, there you have it. I'm going to the meeting at the residence. I drive through to the capitol, wanting to stop for a burrito, but I know I don't have time. It wouldn't do to keep the president waiting when he needs a meeting. I'll get one on the way home.

I pull into the secret parking for the residence and make my way through security. I'm the last to arrive, but not by much. Must be nice to have that D.C. Metro Police escort though.

I'm ushered into a parlor room with fancy sofas and armchairs all around a big fireplace. Everyone looks at me when I walk in the room. Well, that doesn't feel awkward at all.

I walk over to the only empty seat in the room, and it's on the sofa near Grace, thank God, but it's also within touching distance of Ryan. I decide then and there that the only course of action is to completely pretend like he doesn't exist.

"So what's this party all about?" I ask.

"Black was passed a note during the service," Jake responds. "The man identified himself only as the messenger, but the note is unfortunate."

"What does it say?" I ask, when really what I want to ask is what does it have to do with me? I am 100 percent not cut out for all this cloak and dagger nonsense.

They pass a sheet of paper around the room before it gets to me so that everyone can see it. It's tucked safely in a plastic zip bag, I guess to protect the evidence, but I'm not a cop or super-secret spy, so who knows?

I look at it and wonder if this is some kind of a joke. What the hell does this even mean? I hope it makes sense to everyone else, because I have no earthly idea.

```
The Old Ghost may rise, but
the other will fall for him
  to take flight. The eagle
  and her mate are first to
               go.
```

I smile as nothing other than relief courses through my body. Thank God. This has nothing to do with me. This is fantastic!

"What could you be so happy about?" Ryan growls, making me jump a little in my seat. I look over my shoulder. I had forgotten he was so close.

"I'm not happy," I reply. When he looks like he doesn't believe me, I press on. "Really. I promise. I'm just relieved, because this doesn't have anything to do with me."

"How do you figure?"

"Because I have no idea what it means," I admit. "If I don't know what any of this is, then it can't be about me."

"You're joking?" he snaps, and I look around the room in which everyone is wearing the same shocked expression with their eyebrows in their hairlines.

"No," I say slowly. "I don't think so."

"Honey, it's all about you," Jake says softly.

"What?" I shout.

"And me," he says before a heavy pause, and by the look on his face, I feel like he's trying to quietly tell me something, but I don't know what. "And someone else."

"I don't understand," I admit.

"Let's break it down," Rick says. "The Old Ghost is Jake. Ghost was his SEAL call sign."

"Okay."

"And this says that for him to rise, others will fall."

"I don't like that," I mutter to myself, but it was apparently louder than I meant it to be, because everyone is either smiling or their lips are twitching.

"I don't like it either," Rick says.

"That's great and all, but what does this have to do with me?" I prompt. I know I sound like an asshole for asking, but I really don't get it. And I don't want to. I don't want to be involved in anything or with anyone who is trying to manipulate the president.

"This part right here," Rick says, "is you."

"The eagle and her mate are the first to go?" I read the last bit of the letter. "I don't get it."

"Babe," Ryan clips out, and his tone of voice does absolutely nothing to hide his frustration or the fact that he thinks I'm an absolute moron. Great. "You used to work for Eagle News. The eagle is you."

"What?" I gasp. "Someone wants to kill me?"

"Maybe," Rick admits. "We don't know."

"Well, if someone could find out, that would be fucking great," I snap before I get my emotions in hand. "I'm sorry. I'm just under a lot of stress. I don't mean to be a bitch. Really."

"You're fine, honey," Jake says gently.

"Thanks."

The eagle and her mate are the first to go.

I read it over and over again. And then it clicks. Oh,

thank God. It can't be me. *The eagle and her mate are the first to go.* I don't have a mate! I've never been so glad to be single. I want to fist pump in the air like the end of a cult classic '80s film I'm so excited.

"It can't be me!" I practically shout with glee.

"How do you figure that?" Ryan drawls.

"I'm single! I don't have a mate!" I shout. "Woohoo!"

"Everybody out," Jake orders.

"Jake?" Grace asks.

"Everyone," he confirms. I stand and start to follow everyone out, but he stops me. "Not you."

I don't like where this is going.

Fuck, fuck, fuck.

"Why?" I ask.

"I think you know why," he says gently.

"Are you going to fire me?"

"No." He laughs. "I just want to make sure you're safe."

"Okay."

"I have a buddy who owns a security company," Ryan says, startling me. I had forgotten he was still in the room, even though it makes sense, because Jake apparently thinks he's my mate. I don't know how to tell him that his military adviser just likes to fuck and chuck. God, what a disgusting term that is.

"I don't think it'll come to that," I hedge.

"King is great at his job, and all his guys know what they're doing," he says.

"I'm sure he is," I say. "Still. I'll be careful."

"Julia," he murmurs, and I know he's frustrated with me.

"It's my life, Ryan," I reply gently. "I have a right to live it how I want to."

"We'll see—"

"No, we won't," I snap before turning back to Jake. "Meeting adjourned, now that we've discovered the secrets of the universe?"

"Meeting adjourned," he agrees, and I can see a mischievous twinkle in his eyes. Time to run.

"Well… see you all later." And then I exit as fast as my fancy footwear will take me.

I need cats. Cats are safe.

FRESHMAN
CONGRESSMAN
SEEN DINING
WITH
POWERFUL
SISTER

CHAPTER 14

Settled

I *can do this. I can do this. I can do this.*

I *can't* do this.

Shit. I can do this.

I step out of my car and smooth my palms down the front of my dove-gray sheath dress. Normally, I would walk in through the back entrance of this restaurant so I could eat in peace. The owners are really good about politicians and their staff being able to grab a quiet meal and head back to the capitol.

Not to mention there have been many backdoor deals made in the private dining room in the back. I have never personally witnessed any, but I have heard talk. The owners know how much clientele they would lose if they no longer had those perks. And this isn't a tourist destination.

However, my brother Gil, an up-and-coming congressman in New York, is all about seeing and being seen—that is, as long as he's making the right connections. And his baby sister is the White House Press Secretary, so there are those connections. Anything that can link Gil to the actual White House has him salivating, no doubt.

And he is my only brother. Having been my only friendly ally growing up—when I could count on him—built a soft spot in me for him. He was the only one in the house who showed me any kindness. Where my parents could be cruel and exacting in what they wanted from me, Gil was always ready with a happy smile and a charming story about his day. I don't know where I would be without that. Probably some sad society wife with a prescription pill addiction and a husband who fucks anything that moves. Somehow, knowing there were good things out there in the world made me want to go out and see them and experience them for myself. Not that I didn't have a charmed life. I did. I had anything and everything money could buy. And the kind of old money my family has meant I had everything.

It just wasn't anything of substance.

I wanted my life to mean something. So I majored in journalism instead of something useless for my M-R-S degree. I knocked on door after door so I could get the best internships, and then I rocked my interviews and got jobs with great networks. I know that doesn't typically happen right off the bat, but I believe it was a combination of both luck and hard work. It was hard work that put me at NYU, and it was luck that led to Grace, Angie, and me being roommates. It was hard work that got me to Eagle News, but it was luck that got my name in front of a senator running for President.

So when Gil called this morning and asked to meet for an early dinner, I said yes. I said yes, because I love my brother, since he was the only one who loved me in that house of horrors. And I said yes knowing he would not want me to sneak in the back entrance to have a private dinner with my only sibling. I knew Gil would expect me to come in the front entrance, where anyone could see me, including the paparazzi, who he would have called, and then dine next to the big glass windows, where we could be seen and photographed looking fabulous and like the next Kennedy family.

"Jules!" someone shouts as I approached the door to the restaurant. "Is it true?"

I just smile politely as a hostess from the establishment opens the door for me.

"Good evening, Ms. Fairchild. Your table is right this way," she says as she leads me to a table next to the front window. It looks like it has an excellent view of the city, but it can also be seen from the front of the building, which sits on a corner lot.

"Thank you," I reply.

"Julia," Gil says, standing as I approach the table. "You look lovely as always."

"Thank you, brother dear." I pop a kiss to his cheek and let him help me with my chair.

I unfold my napkin and drop it in my lap. I know the menu by heart here, so I know exactly what I'm going to get, and I've been looking forward to it all day. Not to mention, this is my first time out of my house during my imposed isolation to avoid the media. Although that doesn't mean I haven't seen Ryan. And I mean I've seen *all* of Ryan over the last few nights. I just can't help myself.

"So what's good here?" Gill asks. "Everyone swears this is the place to go to in D.C."

"It's fantastic," I tell him. "I eat here at least three times a month."

"Are you ready to order?" a waitress asks as she steps up to our table with a smile on her face.

"I am if you are, Gil."

"Sure," he says good-naturedly. "You go first, and I'll be ready by the end."

"I'll have the chicken napoleon please," I say, handing the waitress my menu. It's this amazing chicken and mushrooms in a creamy sundried tomato sauce over penne pasta with cheeses melted on top. I get it every time I come here.

"Is that wise?" Gil asks me under his breath.

"And a house salad to start," I add, rolling my eyes.

"Better." He chuckles. "I'll have the grilled chicken and steamed vegetables," he orders. "No sauce, no rice or pasta."

"Coming right up," she says before walking away, and I can barely hold back the disgusted look on my face. Why anyone would order food that boring, I have no idea.

"What?" He laughs. "It's not so bad."

"Not so bad?" I ask in a mock shocked tone.

"It's healthy," he replies with a smile on his face. "It wouldn't look good if I got a gut. You could probably use to eat a vegetable every now and then too."

"What's that supposed to mean?" I ask quietly. This is the first time Gil has even been critical of me outwardly in any way, and I'm not sure I like it.

"It just means I love you, and I want you to be healthy and live a long time," he says.

"Well, I'll have you know I eat boring food like that all the time, but this is the one place I let myself have my favorite meal."

"Good," he says softly, patting my hand where it rests on the table. "You should have something that brings you joy."

"There are a lot of things that bring me joy in my life," I tell him as the waitress sets my salad down in front of me.

"Like what?" he asks as I push the lettuce, tomatoes, cheese, and croutons covered in dressing around on my plate.

"I love my job," I admit, taking a bite and chewing

thoughtfully. "I love my friends, and I'm very close with them. I'm even planning a trip to visit Angie in Texas."

"But you have nothing of your own," he says, and I have to admit it stings. Hearing my beloved brother voice my own inner demons does not feel good. I had always considered my life to be full, but now that I'm living a life in half measures with Ryan, I can't help but wonder if that's really the truth after all.

"I have a full life," I explain. "Cara's daughter Rachel is at such a fun age, and Grace is having a baby this year. Not to mention, Angie has Joy."

"But those are their children. Don't you want any of your own some day?" he asks as the waitress sets out meals down in front of us.

"I do," I admit as I toy with my dinner. "Someday."

Cabe and Lacy slam into my brain. Ryan is twelve years older than I am. He has two children who are practically grown and out of the house and an ex-wife who he's still friends with. His life is full. Obviously, there isn't room for me in it, the way he bounces out of my bed with his boots already on every evening and then out the door. And even if there was room, he already has two kids. He won't want any more. I need to cut my losses. Maybe in a few years, I can adopt a baby from overseas. This is the twenty-first century. I don't have to be married to a man to have a baby. I can do it myself.

"Don't you want to settle down and have a family?" Gil prods carefully as he skillfully cuts into his chicken.

"Sometimes," I respond, shrugging. "I don't know. What about you?"

"I'm going to marry a woman who will compliment me and my career," he says like it's the most logical choice. "As soon as I win this next election cycle, I'll choose someone. Actually, I hear there's a great matchmaker here for politically elevated families."

"But don't you want more?" I blurt, and I swear an annoyed look flits across his face, but it's gone before I can be sure. "Don't you want a love match?"

"What good will that do me?" He laughs. "I need someone who can go the distance so I can sit in your boss's office in a few years. Besides, who's to say we won't grow to love each other? Does that surprise you?"

"Yeah, I guess it does," I say before taking another bite of pasta. Suddenly, my favorite meal tastes like ash in my mouth. "I always thought you were different."

"I am different, honey," he says gently. "But I'm also practical. You were the dreamer. I want the White House, and to do that, I need to be well-connected to strong political allies."

"Okay," I say.

"So you understand?"

"Yes, Gil," I reply sadly. "I understand."

"Thank you," he says, closing his eyes for a second before opening them. "I was hoping you'd say that."

"Of course. I'll always support my favorite brother," I reply cheekily.

"Great," he says, his voice full of feeling. "So you'll have dinner with Senator Chancellor?"

"Wait, what?" I ask.

"You'll help me make those political allies by aligning with the president's father."

"Not so fast," I hiss over the table quietly. "I said I would support you in making your political allies. I will not marry a man I do not love, especially one old enough to be my grandfather."

"But you said you wanted a family of your own one day," he rallies. "Kids? How are you ever going to have kids if you don't settle down?"

"And you think a man in his early eighties wants to have babies running around?" I laugh. "I don't think so. I mean, his own son is in his forties."

"You said it yourself," he challenges. "That you're excited about Grace's baby. "You'll make a wonderful grandmother to that baby."

"This is insane," I whisper-yell at him. "I won't do it."

"Please," he begs. "I need this connection."

"You'll have to make it another way," I say sadly. "I can't be bought."

"We'll see about that," he mutters under his breath,

and I raise my hand and ask for a box. I'm going to go back to my house and binge this entire plate of pasta and whatever *Real Housewives* franchise or *Cash Cab* I can on demand tonight. There's a bottle of wine and some yoga pants with my name on them. "Julia, you have to see reason."

"What I see is that you're so much like them now," I say as I box up my dinner. "I love you, and I always will, but this hurts."

"You're being childish and unreasonable," he snaps.

"I'm being childish?" I ask. "You called me and set up this dinner to look good for the papers. Don't pretend like this whole evening had anything to do with me."

"I love you, Julia," he says with a sigh as he stands to hug me. When he pulls me close, he says in my ear, "Don't make a foolhardy mistake that we'll both regret."

"I won't," I reply quietly when I pull away.

"Just… think on it, will you?"

"Yeah," I agree for lack of anything better to say. It's a lie, and I think we both know it is. I won't ever consider selling my body to a man I don't love, let alone trust, just so my brother can one day be president. Those are his aspirations, not mine.

I pick up my takeout box and my purse from the table and head out into the camera flashes of the local media with a fake smile on my face. I'm barely through the door when someone bumps into me and practically slams me into the ground, when I'm swept into a set of arms.

"Excuse me," I say until I look up at who has a hold of me, and then I want to throw up.

"Fancy bumping into you here," Senator Chancellor says as he smiles brightly at me.

The media all around us is chomping at the bit for pictures and answers to questions. There's not a damn thing I can do right now, because I've been expertly caught in his trap, one that's very similar to the one his son set for his own wife. He's much too powerful in the political arena, still, for me to take on all on my own. I'm going to have to wait and see if I can undo the trap that he so skillfully set for me.

Carefully, I extricate myself from his arms with a polite but in no way inviting smile on my face and then head in the direction of my car. I'm seething by the time I beep the locks on my key fob and drop down into the driver seat.

I thought I was having dinner with my brother.

I was sure I was being used.

I had absolutely no idea he was setting me up for a fall.

I drive myself home like a little old lady, although in hindsight, maybe a reckless driving ticket would have made me less appealing to the president's father. Who knows? I toss my dress in the dry-cleaning bag, even though I contemplate burning it or throwing it in the trash, and pull on my ugly period sweats and eat my leftovers in bed, leaving the carton on the night-stand. I'll pick it up tomorrow, when I'm on my way back to work—that is if this doesn't screw me again.

And then I tuck myself into my covers and promise myself that after work tomorrow, I will adopt eight cats like Grace and never even look at a man ever again. And then I fall asleep, and it won't be until much later that I would realize Ryan never showed.

**PRETTY PRESS
SECRETARY SWEPT OFF
HER FEET BY NEW BEAU**

CHAPTER 15

Armor

I did not see that coming.

This morning when my alarm rang, I felt relieved. I missed being in the office. I thrive on being at the heart of the news day. And to be at the heart of the nation and see first hand the making of that news is awe- inspiring, so even though my personal life is an absolute shambles, I was ready to be back, and I jumped out of bed with excitement and a grateful heart.

I showered and dressed with care in a black suit of skinny-cut slacks, a matching tailored blazer with a peplum waist, and a taupe silk blouse underneath. I dried and curled my hair in soft waves around my shoulders to soften the look and applied tasteful make-up in soft pinks and shimmery golds. I pushed my diamond studs through my ears and wrapped my watch around my wrist, and I stepped into a pair of sky-high

Louboutins.

I know it seems weird and most wouldn't feel the same way, but my heels are my armor. They give me confidence. There's just something empowering about donning a great pair or a red lipstick. It makes me feel bold. And something tells me that after last night, I'm going to need to be bold today. So I'll take my armor in any way it might come.

Even though I was excited to go back to work, it was not without a fair amount of trepidation. Gil and Senator Chancellor set me up last night, plain and simple. I trusted my brother as the only member of my family who deserved my faith in him, and I'm not ready to completely give up on him, but he chose to side with my parents in my current battle, so I need to keep that in mind. Not because Gil can't be trusted, but because the trust I had already given freely—even if a little misguided—is going to cost me, and I won't know just how much until I hit the office this morning and see if I'm still on house arrest.

I stopped in the kitchen and made myself a cup of coffee and a bagel with cream cheese at home. Usually, I'm a breakfast skipper, but I was so excited to start my day that I blew through my preparations in record time.

I still stopped for my latte on my way into the capitol. I parked in my usual spot in the staff lot, and I made my way through security like I always do. I kept to myself, not on purpose but because I was lost in my own head. I didn't notice the weird looks I was getting from the people around me.

I made my way down the hallway and into the staff offices. I fired up my computer and logged in, but I didn't have time to tap into the press wires yet, because my office phone started ringing, bringing me to the now.

"Hello?" I answer.

"Ms. Fairchild, the president needs to see you ASAP," the bitchy secretary says without greeting. Weirdly enough, there's a hint of a smile in her voice that sends a chill down my spine. If she's happy about calling me, things are not going to go my way.

"I'll be right there," I reply before hanging up.

I drop my purse in my desk drawer and secure it, even though there's a strong chance I'm about to be fired. *Shit.* I make my way down the hallway quickly, knowing it won't bode well to keep the president waiting when I'm being called down to the carpet.

The secretary smiles like the cat that got her cream when she sees me, and I feel sick to my stomach. This is not good. Regardless, I look her square in the eye and hold my head high. She smirks but doesn't say anything, and I raise my hand to knock on the door.

"They're waiting for you," she purrs, and I don't look back at her. I let my fist knock on the door.

"Come in," Jake barks from the interior. Shit, shit, shit. He's really mad.

I square my shoulders, push the door open, and step inside.

"Shut the door behind you," he orders, and I catch the bitch's eye as I turn and close the door. She's smiling full-out now, and I want to throw up.

"You wanted to see me," I say, and I'm proud of the fact that there's only a hint of a tremor to be heard in my voice. I look around, and the room isn't full, but it's not empty either. Jake, Ryan, Rick, and Gus all stand around. They are an intimidating group of men, I'm not going to lie, but I'm a badass too.

"There's something you need to see, Jules," Rick says softly.

"If it's photos of me leaving a restaurant last night," I begin and look to Jake, "you should know that while I haven't seen them, I know it was a setup. I was there to have dinner with my brother, Gil, and your father waylaid me on the way out. It was a photo op ambush."

"This isn't photos, Jules," Jake says, and I tip my head to the side, letting my confusion show on my face.

"If it's not photos, then what is it?" I ask.

"Come here," Rick says, handing me an iPad.

I press Play and watch as my entire life implodes.

"Ohhh... yes. Yes!"

I watch as a strong, masculine hand—Ryan's hand—thrusts two fingers into my pussy. My hips arch up to meet him. Swirling wisps of color tease and twirl around his arm in the form of a tattoo, but from this angle, you can't tell what it is in the video. But I clearly have firsthand knowledge of the soldier's cross tattoo that sits on that tan stretch of skin.

"Please!" I hear myself beg. And oh, how I've begged for this man's touch. The way he burns me up from the inside out should be criminal.

"Mmm." He chuckles, low and throaty, because he was enjoying teasing me, keeping me on the edge. He always loves to torture me, to touch me, and to fuck me. It's weird standing here, watching this all play out with him standing on the opposite side of the room.

"Please!" I needed him so badly. Truth be told, I still do, and thankfully, he's inclined to oblige me, because he shows up in the middle of the night almost every night. Even now that I've sworn off men, I know that if he comes to me again, I would let him inside me, and I would beg him to do it.

My cheeks heat, and I try to clench my thighs without anyone noticing, but he notices. I see him smirk out the corner of my eye. He knows what he does to me and how well he does it too. There has never been, and I know in my heart of hearts that there never will be another man who knows my body and how to play it like Ryan Black does.

I watch the screen as he grips his thick, veiny cock in his fist before rubbing the flushed tip through my wetness and then up to stroke my clit, making me bite my lip to keep from crying out, because my torture only seems to egg him on. The higher my passion climbs, the more turned on he gets. Ryan seems to thrive on pleasing me, at least in bed. In life, I'm not so sure.

It's weird being both humiliated and turned on in a roomful of your friends and colleagues, but it's also nothing I'm new to. I had a full career as a primetime news anchor. You don't make it that far without a few scars on your arms and knives in your back. Although, even I have to admit this one takes the cake.

My parents are going to kill me. Whatever reprieve I bought myself by blocking them has now been laid to waste. Good news is, I can't see Senator Chancellor wanting to marry me anymore after this. At least that's one line item I can check off on my "Julia Fairchild's Epic Lemons to Lemon Vodka Life List."

"Ahhh," I moan as he finally notches the very tip of him at my center and slides in all the way. That sound is embarrassing. It's a high keening sound kind of like a cat in heat, although I guess that's what I was. The knowledge that Ryan can turn me into an animal is not a happy one.

"Kill me now," I mumble under my breath, and I watch as he shifts his weight from one foot to the other. It's a subtle gesture, but it's also a telling one. He's not as unaffected as he seems. Good. He should feel as hot and bothered as I do.

I remember the moment so well, not only because he showed me a repeat performance the other night, but because it was that memorable. He had my body strung so tight and pushed me higher and higher. I was like a lit fuse on a bomb.

The muscles in his thighs and ass flex and ripple as he pulls out to the tip only to thrust back in, making my tits bounce like a porn star. Is that what I am now? A porn star? He grips my hips so tight in his hands that I wore marks for days, just like the ones I carry on my skin now under my slacks.

I feel my eyes glaze over. I'm lost in the moment, watching as he pumps into me over and over again. I watch as my hands grip the sheets of the hotel bed tight as I arch my back while he fucks me into oblivion.

And then I watch with everyone else as my jaw drops down on a silent scream and my eyes close when I find completion in the mystery man's arms.

Jake clears his throat. "I think we've seen enough," he says uncomfortably, and I hit Pause on the iPad.

"The video was released thirty-seven minutes ago," Rick says. "And has been viewed twenty-six million times."

Jesus Christ.

There's a knock at the door.

"Come in," Jake says.

"I was looking for Jules," my assistant says as he pokes his head in the room. "The Press Room is ready for you to brief them on HB 2250."

"Great," I say, not feeling it at all. I kind of feel like throwing up. In fact, I think I might.

"You don't have to go in there, Jules," Jake says gently. "We can send in someone else. Hell, I'll do it myself."

"Normally, I would say no to that," Rick adds. "But

for you, I'd even do it."

"Come on, guys." I laugh, but it lands flat even to my own ears. "This happens every day. I'll be old news by tomorrow. Time to get back on the horse."

"Jules, you don't have to be brave in here," Jake tells me. He knows me well for someone who's new to my life. Marrying my bestie, Grace, was the smartest thing he ever did, and he loves her so much he'd do anything for her. Including protect her idiot best friend from a sex tape scandal.

I shrug one shoulder like it's no big deal. "Nah, I can't let them smell my fear. Besides, I'm surprised it hasn't happened before now."

And then I walk out of the Oval Office and down the hall toward the White House Press Room to brief a bunch of great white sharks on a Congressional Bill that the president vehemently opposes and—plot twist—all while my boobs are bouncing around the internet like a porn star and the knowledge that the world has now seen my "O" face.

"Good morning, ladies and gentlemen," I say, stepping up to the podium in the press room. "Let's talk about the elephant in the room."

The cacophony of sound from everyone jumping to their feet and shouting their questions at me is overwhelming, but I don't let it startle me. In fact, it calms me down. This is my zone. I'm in my element, and here, no one can hurt me.

"Quiet and I'll get to your questions in a minute,"

I order, and they settle a little, but I can tell they're chomping at the bit. "This morning, a tape was published to the internet. A tape of me and a gentleman in an intimate setting. This tape was made without my knowledge or consent and also without that of the gentleman in the tape. It is currently under investigation. That is all I know at this time."

"Jules!" someone shouts. "Who's the man?"

"That question, I will not answer… ever," I say calmly.

"Come on, Jules. That's not fair."

"What's not fair is a private citizen of the United States having his nude body in a very private setting blasted all over the internet for mass consumption," I reply sternly. "He is not for you to pick apart over and over."

"Don't you think we deserve to know his identity, since he's involved with a public figure?"

"No, I do not," I answer. "Also, he and I are no longer involved, so that's a nonstarter. Next question."

"Senator Chancellor has publicly claimed that it is him in the video," someone shouts. "Can you confirm that?"

Now that surprises me. Damn. Double damn. I had thought this video would finally get him off my back, but apparently it just made him double down.

I smile before I answer. "Have you seen the tape?" I ask the reporter who posed the question.

"Yes."

"Does that look like the body of an eighty-year-old man to you?"

"No," he answers to the sound of snickers all around the room.

"The senior senator is in great shape, no doubt," I reply. "But I have no carnal knowledge of him or his body. So I will repeat one more time for the people in the back. I have not now or ever been romantically or intimately involved with the president's father, nor will I. We are not engaged, and we are not getting married."

"I thought your family supported the match?"

"They may support the match," I answer, "but that doesn't mean a match is happening. While in that vein, I will not be commenting on the inner dynamics of my family and personal life. Now, does anyone have any questions about House Bill 2250?"

THE MOAN HEARD ROUND THE WORD:

Press Secretary Sex Tape
Beats Out Reality Star for
Top Views in Minutes

CHAPTER 16

Cornered

I finally wrap up the press conference and leave the room with my head held high and a stiff upper lip. My life might have gone to hell in a handbasket, but I'm not going to let it get me down.

One step at a time.

I know there will be even more press camped out at my house, even more questions, because I didn't give them the whole story, and I will not. Besides, it's none of their goddamn business.

I make my way back down the hall toward my office, when suddenly, I'm grabbed by the arm and pulled into a dark, vacant office. The door closes behind us with a snick, and I'm pushed against the wall. I open my mouth to let out a scream, but a large hand covers my mouth.

"Hush." I instantly still at the sound of a voice I recognize. "Are you going to scream if I move my hand?"

I shake my head, and he moves his hand, but he does not step away from where he has me pinned with his body against the wall in a dark room.

"Ryan?" I whisper.

"Yeah, babe."

"Why did you kidnap me?" I ask quietly.

"I need some answers," he responds cryptically.

"Okay."

"What the fuck was that?"

"What the fuck was what?" I ask, even though I'm pretty sure I already know the answer to the question.

"The tape?" he thunders in hushed tones.

"I didn't make it," I say, and anger pours through my body and I see red at his accusation. "Wait a minute. Do you think I made it?"

"Babe, you have to see that is the logical conclusion."

"You're really something, you know that?" I snap as I realize that like all the men—hell, all the people, period, end of—in my family, Ryan is just fucking like them. Not one person thinks I might just be a decent human being with hopes and dreams, thoughts and feelings of my own. Everyone is out to use me or expects to be used, and it's disgusting.

"Jules—" he starts, but I don't let him finish. I buck against him.

"Let me go," I demand, because I can't stand to be in this room, this close to him, for a minute longer.

"Jules, listen—"

"No," I snap. Suddenly, I'm close to tears. My emotions are riding me hard, and I can't help it, but what I can help is the situation. It's time I start standing up for myself. I can't be Ryan's doormat any longer. "I need you to let me go."

"Honey, stop," he says, but I don't care. I fight harder. I need to get away from here, from him, from his soft voice that makes me purr like a kitten.

"No."

"Stop," he commands. "Before you hurt yourself."

"No!" I cry. "You stop. You're hurting me."

He instantly lets me go at my words.

"Baby, please."

"No," I repeat, wrapping my arms around my waist. "I'm not strong enough for this. No more hon-eyed words or pet names, no more late-night trysts, and no more dark office conversations. I'm not this person. There is no duplicitous bone in my body. You may think I'm that kind of political mercenary, that I would take a video of us on a night, I'll remind you, that you instigated, and I tried to avoid. And then you feel like I'm the kind of woman who would then publish a vid-eo of an intimate, private moment between us for some reason that I'm not sure of. So we're done, here and anywhere. I can't do it anymore."

"Are you done?" he asks me.

"Well… yeah."

"Good, then it's my turn," he says, and I feel my belly drop into my shoes. This is not good, and I need to get out of here.

"Ryan," I whisper. I can hear the panic in my voice, and by the white flash of his smile in the dark, I can tell he hears it too. I need to get out of here like yesterday. I should have gone on safari when I had the chance and never came back, and now it's too late. "Let me go."

"No," he says as he presses in. He crowds me against the wall again, and the hard heat of his body presses into mine. He has me cornered, and I have nowhere to go. "You had your chance to talk, and now it's mine."

"I… uhh…" I stammer and then lick my lips. His eyes drop down to my mouth and heat before they flit back up to my eyes again. "I think we covered everything we need to."

"See," he says, pressing closer still, "I don't think that we did."

"Well, I do."

"You had your say, and now it's my turn," he begins once more, and I open my mouth to form a rebuttal, but he stops me with a hand low on my belly. "I will admit that, for a second, I considered you may have orchestrated this whole thing, but now I know for sure you did not."

"How can you be sure?"

"I'm sure," he says. "You also have to admit that this will harm me more than it will harm you."

"What do you mean?" I ask, and I'm not sure why, but I do not like the idea of anything hurting Ryan, even if he did hurt me.

"Honey, celebrities weather this kind of storm all the time," he says gently. "You'll be fine."

"Yeah, and…?"

"I'm not a celebrity," he answers.

"I don't understand."

"Think about it, Jules," Ryan starts. "I'm a military man. When my identity in that video gets out, I'll be court martialed."

"What?" I gasp. I don't know much about the military, but I do know that a court martial is not a good thing. I thought it was only for big criminals, but I might be wrong.

"This kind of conduct is not befitting of an officer," he explains gently. "I will be tried and convicted, and then my military career will be over."

"No."

"Yes," he presses on. "So you have to forgive me for the two seconds I had to weigh all the facts that I know so far. And I really am sorry you were hurt by any part of that."

"It's okay," I whisper. "But you have to know, I won't tell."

"Honey, you have to," he says. "They'll eat you alive if you don't."

"Ha!" I laugh, suddenly finding my confidence again. "This is my world. The hive doesn't eat the queen, and I am the queen bee here."

"Okay, well how about the fact that I'm not the kind of guy who will let his woman take the fall for him?" he prompts, knocking some of the wind from my sails for a variety of reasons.

"Let's start at the beginning with that one," I tell him. "One, I'm not your woman."

"You are."

"I am not."

"You are," he says again.

"Take it back."

"No."

"Fine," I snap. "If I'm your woman, why do you leave me every time? You treat me like a hit it and quit it."

He seems stunned for a moment, and then his smile is huge and blinding. "I was trying to give you space. I had no idea you wanted me to stay."

"I don't. But you still left!" Shit, I'm letting all of my cards show on the table. I can't let Ryan know how much he affects me. This is so not good.

"Honey," he says, his voice whiskey-smooth. "I was trying to protect you."

"Protect me?" I ask, and if he said anything else, it wouldn't have surprised me more.

"I was afraid that if our courtship, which you have to admit has been rocky—"

"That's the understatement of the century," I mutter under my breath, but he hears it, and I know he does, because his hand at my belly slides around to my hip and it hard and quick in warning.

"—and I was afraid that if I didn't get you settled and good and used to the idea of a you and me before that played out in the media, then it would be an absolute clusterfuck."

"And now it's playing out in the media," I add helpfully.

"And it's an absolute clusterfuck."

"But they don't know who you are."

"Not yet, at least," he says with a heavy sigh. "But I think they'll figure it out real quick when we're seen in public together."

"Not happening."

"Oh, it's happening," he says, his voice low. "I haven't wanted anyone like this in years, if ever, and I'm not going to come this far only to have you slip through my fingers now."

"You just want a fuck buddy. I'm sure any woman will do," I mumble and instantly regret my words. I wish I had never let them fall out of my mouth, because if he agrees with me, I'm not sure how I'll cope with the knowledge.

"Wrong."

"What?" I whisper.

"It's you," he says. "I don't want a fuck buddy. I want you. All of you. In and out of bed."

"You can't be serious."

"I'm about as serious as a heart attack," he growls. "Now, I'm going to kiss the fuck out of you, and then we're going to sneak out of this office, which chafes against everything I am, and we will continue this conversation tonight after I've sank my cock so deep inside you that you forget where I end and you begin."

"Ryan," I gasp.

"This is happening," he says.

"But—" I try again. My heart is racing so fast it feels like it's going to beat right out of my chest. I feel like my life is now wild and out of control, and the wild has 100 percent to do with Ryan Black.

"This is happening," he repeats in a low, gentle voice, and then he touches his mouth to mine, licking at the seam of my lips. I gasp, and he pushes his tongue inside to tangle with mine. I hold onto his shoulders for dear life.

And then the kiss is over just as fast as it began. Which is probably for the best, because it wouldn't do for us to be caught making out in a vacant office if I'm going to protect him and his career from scandal and ruin.

"I'll see you tonight," he says just before he gently kisses me one last time.

And then he's gone.

How does he keep doing that?

WHO IS THE MAN IN THE VIDEO? INQUIRING MINDS WANT TO KNOW!

CHAPTER 17

Be with me

"*How could you do this to us?*"

After my invasive press conference, no one wanted to discuss the bill that the president openly opposes but Congressman Grissom seems hellbent on passing, so I decided enough was enough and called an end to the workday.

Not to mention Ryan said "we were happening" and that he would be at my house tonight, so I decided to batten down the hatches. I was determined to find how he was getting in my house and to put a stop to it. He's not magic. He can't walk through walls. Can he?

So I grabbed my purse from my office and locked up for the evening. I kept my head held high and my chin up and dared anyone with my eyes to stare at me as I moved through the offices and hallways. I have done nothing wrong, and I refuse to behave like I have something to be sorry for, because I absolutely do not.

I made my way back through security and out to the staff parking lot, where I climbed in my car and headed toward home. I drove through the Taco Bell drive-thru near my house and ordered the giant two chalupas and a taco meal, because if there was ever a day that one could indulge in junk food, it's a day like today.

Now, I pull into the garage, not wanting to deal with all of the news vans camped on my front lawn, but at the same time knowing I will have to eventually. I turn the car off, grab my purse and my takeout bag, and shut the garage door before locking the door and walking in the house.

I kick off my heels and set my purse and takeout bag on the kitchen island, when my cell phone rings.

"Hello?" I answer.

"Honey, are you all right?" Grace asks.

"I'll be fine," I tell her. "Really."

"You know we can be on a yacht in the Greek Sea by two tomorrow," she says with a smile in her voice.

"I've already been the cause of a national incident," I droll. "I will not be the cause of an international one too."

"Party pooper." She laughs. "But seriously. If you need me, I'm there."

"I know," I tell her. "But really. I'll be all right."

"Taco Bell?" she asks.

"And Tequila."

"Got it. Go conquer the world," she says and then hangs up.

I head upstairs and slip out of my clothes and put on a pair of men's style sweatpants that have baggy legs that gather at the ankles and a tank top. I pull wool socks on my feet and make my way back downstairs.

I eat a chalupa while standing at the kitchen counter and look around the room. How could he be getting in? But I get distracted by the blinking red light on my answering machine. I know it's old-fashioned and not many people have landlines and answering machines anymore, but I do. I like the feeling of being connected.

I wad up my wrapper and reach for another as I hit the Play button on my machine and instantly regret it when the hateful tone of my mother's voice fills the room.

"How could you do this to us?" she screeches. *"We are so embarrassed by you. No, we're not embarrassed; we're humiliated!"*

I take a bite of my second chalupa while she continues her tirade over my lack of decorum and class. I shrug. It is what it is. It would have been nice to have a family who rallies around me when I need them during a crisis like this, but again, it is what it is. You can't miss what you never had.

"You're just lucky Jefferson is willing to look past this," she says. *"He's still willing to have you and goddammit, you listen and you listen well. You will do the right thing for this family or there will be consequenc-*

es."

I snort. There's literally nothing she can do to me. She has nothing to hold over my head anymore. I'm thirty-five years old and have a fantastic career and plenty of savings. *She* should worry about *me*. I could easily write a tell-all. Although I would never do that to my brother, Gil, no matter how mad I am at him right now.

Another message clicks over, and Gil's concerned voice fills the room. I guess speak of the devil. Say his name and he shall appear on your answering machine.

"Jules, what's going on?" he asks. *"I'm worried about you. Give me a call."*

I sigh. I'll give him a call when I'm ready, but for tonight, I just want to hunker down and lick my wounds. And with that thought, I drop my half eaten chalupa on the counter. I'm no longer hungry. I fill a glass with water from the kitchen tap and chug it down before placing the glass in the sink. I'll deal with this mess later.

I make my way into the living room, pull my lilac throw from the back of the sofa, and wrap it around me. I lie down on my side across the sofa with my back against the cushions. A shuddered breath forces its way out of my chest, and then the first tear rolls down my cheek. Then another and another.

It's dark by the time I've had a good cry, and the room is filled with shadows, since I didn't turn on any lights in this room, but I don't care. I just want to be alone with my thoughts. I can't conquer the world until I conquer what's inside my brain first. But my dark thoughts are interrupted by my sexy nighttime intruder, reminding me that I forgot all about my quest to figure out how he gets in night after night.

"Babe, this shit on your counter will kill you," he says from the doorway that connects the two rooms. I jump up from the sofa. I'm sure my eyes are wild, and I know my heart is racing.

"W-w-what are you doing here?" I stammer as I clutch my blanket around me like a cloak.

He stares at me for a beat before answering. "I told you that I would be here."

"Oh… that's right," I mumble. "How do you get in?"

"I have my ways," he tells me as he stalks into the room.

"I think you should tell me what those ways are," I say out loud and then think, *so I can stop them.*

"Not yet," he says. "Come here."

"No."

"I'm really thinking you should come here," he says gently.

"No."

"Then I'll come to you," he says, taking another step closer.

"No!" I blurt.

"Why not?" Ryan asks casually as he stills his movements. He's totally in tune with me, and I equal parts love it, because no one has ever completely seen me like he does, and hate it, because he sees everything, and I can hide nothing.

"Kids!" I practically word vomit on the rug in front of me and wish I hadn't shown something so important to me, but Gil's words ring in my head. Ryan is twelve years older than me with two mostly grown children. He isn't going to want to have babies with me, not that we're there in our relationship.

"What about kids?" he asks me. Actually, maybe this is good. Maybe I can make him see we're a bad match and he needs to walk away, that we have to end this dangerous game we're playing before my heart is engaged as much as my body is and I can't take it back.

"You have them," I explain.

"Yeah," he says, and I don't take notice that his body went dangerously still. He's alert and waiting to see what I say next. I should have paid more attention that I was on precarious waters in a dinghy.

"You have them," I push on. "You've already raised them. I want them. Someday. Maybe soon, I don't know. But you've already done that. So you see? We have to break up."

"What?" he asks. "Why?"

"Because," I explain again. "You've already done that. I haven't. So we can't be together, because I want them. I'm going to adopt. I don't need a man to adopt."

"What about a sperm donor?" he asks, and I shrug my shoulders.

"I could do that too. I haven't thought it all out yet."

"What about me?"

"What about you?"

"Baby, you've had my cum inside you more times than I can count," he explains in his usual brutality.

"What?" I gasp.

"Not once have we used protection," he explains. "You could be carrying my baby in your belly right now."

"What?" I shout.

"And that wouldn't be a bad thing."

"Stop talking," I order, but he doesn't listen. Ryan never listens.

"Baby, I was either in the field or overseas while Kristen was raising our kids," he says gently. "That's a big part of why our marriage failed, and I have not hidden those truths from you. But I would do it again in a heartbeat for the chance to get to be more involved. If it was with you."

"What?" I gasp as he steps closer.

"I think we need to get a few things straight," he says as he carefully pulls me into him and wraps his arms around me.

"Like what?" I whisper.

"I like you, Jules," he tells me gently. "A lot."

"Ryan—"

"And I know you're scared, but we'll work through that."

"I… uhh…." But I don't get the chance to say anything else, because he lightly touches his lips to mine. When he feels me melt into his body, only then does he deepen the kiss.

Ryan ends the kiss and lets me go, but only to take my hand and lead me back to the sofa, where he sits down right smack in the middle with his long legs spread wide. He looks strong and utterly masculine sitting on my prissy sofa, and it's distracting.

That is until he begins to tenderly rub his hands up and down my arms. The soft motion starts to relax the muscles in my body, and without words I gentle toward him again.

He tucks his fingers in the waistband of my sweatpants and slides them down my legs. I step out of them, and he kicks them aside, leaving me in nothing but a tank and a pair of cotton panties with thick lace trim at the waist.

I watch as his eyes heat when he sees me, but he banks the fire for the time being. He takes my hand again and leads me to lay over his lap on my belly. I wonder what he's doing when he cradles me with one arm and then begins to massage my back with his free hand. Ryan kneads the tension from my back and shoulders, and I start to purr like a kitten.

He strokes down my back, each pass taking him

closer and closer to my backside, but he doesn't touch it. He grazes the lace trim of my panties, and then his hand moves back up to my shoulders, only to make another teasing pass.

"I like these," he says, his voice deeper with his arousal as he plays with the edge of the leg of my panties.

"I can tell," I reply quietly. And I can. His hard length is pressing into my belly. It's not uncomfortable in the least. And I get a secret thrill that my utterly not sexy comfy clothes turn him on. They're just cotton panties, nothing fancy, but still, Ryan seems to appreciate them.

He lets go of them and goes back to stroking my lower back. Over and over, only this time, he lets his heavy palm glide down over my ass and then back up again. Each pass he makes takes him farther and farther down my backside.

I gasp when his fingers glide over my pussy. They're there and then they're gone. He moves back up to my shoulders again, teasing me with hints as he makes a random pass over my center every so often, and I begin to press my backside high in the air, hoping Ryan will take the hint without words.

He cups me between my legs with his palm. "In case you didn't get it, I really like these."

I don't reply to his words, but I know I smile a cat that got her cream smile, and I tuck my face into his elbow so he won't see it.

He slides his hand down the back of my panties and brushes over my clit and through my wetness. There's no denying how turned on I am now. And he knows it too, if his deep groan is anything to go by.

Ryan slides his hand out of my panties and then tugs them down my hips. I spread my legs as wide as my panties still around my thighs will allow, and he does not disappoint when he plunges two fingers deep inside me.

"Yes," I pant as he fucks me with his fingers.

I grip his thigh in my hands for leverage and push up so I can rock my hips back against his hand. He pushes down the front of my tank so my breasts are exposed, and the cool air of the room stings against my overheated skin, but it only serves to drive me higher and higher.

He catches my breast as it swings while I rock harder and faster against him, and he cups it in his fist. The feel of the calluses on his hand abrades my skin in the best of ways. He slides his hand across my torso and pinches the nipple on my other breast, and I have to dig my nails into his thigh to ground myself, but it's no use. I'm flying high.

While I'm still coming, Ryan picks me up and plants me on my hands and knees on the sofa, and I drop down so that my face is pressed into the cushions, unable to hold myself up any longer.

And then he's right behind me. I feel him working at his belt and the fly of his jeans, and then he is right there. He drives into me with one quick thrust. I let out a moan at the full feeling of him inside me, stretching me all at once.

Something in him seems to snap at my reaction, because he grips my hips hard in his hands as he pumps in and out of me, harder and faster. He's lost his tight grip on his control, and I revel in it.

"Yes!" I chant as I whip my head back and press into him. He grips my hair and pulls me up on my hands so I'm closer to him, and he crushes his mouth to mine. I open immediately under him and let him plunder my mouth while he continues to fuck me on the sofa.

And then it builds and builds. It's going to roll over me again, and I feel my walls tighten around him.

"Yes," I gasp as I drop back down to press my chest against the cushions, and the rough knit of the material abrades my already sensitive nipples. It's too much and not enough, and I cry out my demands. "Harder. Fuck me harder."

"Yes," he growls as he plunges faster and faster, driving us both close to the edge. "Fuck."

"Harder," I whimper as I dig my nails into the cushions and hold on. "Please. Harder."

He pounds into me, and then I come.

"Fuck," he bites out as he drives deep again and again. "Yes, baby." And then he plants himself deep inside me and follows me into oblivion.

We lie there on the sofa, his front to my back and

his body covering mine while our breaths saw in and out of our bodies. Sex with Ryan has always been fantastic, but this was… more. This was raw, and it was real. It was need, and it was frustration. And I have the feeling that it signifies a major change in our standard operating procedure.

Before I have a chance to put too much thought into it, he pushes up onto his knees and pulls out. He stands beside the sofa, and I feel him looking down at me, but I don't turn my head to confirm it, because even though he's said over and over that we're happening, I can't help but wonder if now that he's had an orgasm if he's going to pull up his pants and leave like he usually does. And I know he said he was protecting me, but still, in my heart of hearts, I always wish he'd just stay.

I don't have to wait too long, because he tenderly places his hands on me and rolls me to my back. And then he scoops me up like a bride and carries me up the stairs to my bedroom, where he places me delicately in the center of the bed and shimmies the covers out from under me.

I watch as he takes off his dog tags, puts them in his pocket, and strips off his clothes. His hard cock still springs free from the parted material of his jeans, which he shoves down his legs and steps out of.

And then he crawls up the bed and covers my body with his. I let my legs open, and he falls between them before rising up on his forearms to take his weight off me. I feel the heat of him at my center, and he looks in my eyes as he slowly slides deep inside.

I wrap my arms and legs around him and hold him to me, while he tenderly glides in and out of my body. He gently touches his lips to mine, and we breathe each other in, but we never close our eyes. Instead, we hold that connection while we connect in other ways, in every way imaginable.

This time is different.

Before, it was wild and out of control like a forest fire. Now, the fire is still there, but it's banked. This is not about need and frustration, instead a deeper emotion, one I'm not ready to put a name to.

He rocks us slowly together, like a boat on calm seas, and then, with our eyes locked, and wrapped up in each other's arms, he takes us there again, and we both find completion together.

"Be with me," he whispers against my mouth. Our bodies are still entwined and joined in the most intimate of ways.

"What?" I whisper back.

"Be with me," he says again, this time stronger. "Be with me in all the ways that matter. I want to be with you during the day and in the light, where we don't hide it away. I want you to get to know my kids and them you. And then when the time is right, I want to give you those babies you want. My babies."

"Ryan," I whimper.

"Say yes."

"Yes."

He closes his eyes in relief and then presses his mouth to mine. He pulls out and rolls, taking me with him so I'm curled in his arms, and he pulls the covers over us.

"Ryan," I say, and I can hear the disappointment in my voice. "You can't stay. Not now."

"I'm going to stay as long as I can," he replies and then kisses me once more. "But first, we have to talk."

"I was afraid you were going to say that." I sigh.

"I think we take the next week for just us but be clear with Jake and Rick what's going on," he says.

"I don't like the idea of having this conversation with my boss."

"Jake knows it's me in the video," Ryan states, rocking my world.

"What?" I gasp.

"Honey, he's known me for years. He knows why I have that tattoo, because he was on the op when it happened."

"Holy shit."

"Yeah," he agrees. "And one day, I'll tell you about it."

"Okay," I say, because I'm not going to pressure him to tell me any of it unless he's ready to. That's his story to tell, not mine.

"I think in a week, we go out."

"Like on a date?" I prompt, and he laughs.

"Yeah, like a date. We should have been dating all along, if I hadn't been behaving like a horse's ass."

"So you want to date me?"

"I want to marry you," he says, making the oxygen in my lungs seize up. "But I think that's going to take some time for you to get used to the idea."

"I think you might be crazy."

"I think you might be right," he admits. "You have to be a little crazy to survive the shit I've seen and come out of it on the other side."

"Okay," I say, changing the subject. "So you want to date."

"Yes," he confirms. "I think we also need to get to the bottom of who is trying to blackmail us into forcing the president's hand."

"I agree."

"I also need to know that you're safe," he says. "Then we can just... be."

"Okay."

"Okay?" he asks, sounding a little unsure, and it makes me feel a little guilty for all the trouble I've given him over the last few months. If we had only been honest with each other from the get-go, then everything would be better off, but also maybe a little less interesting.

"Okay," I say again. "We can't go back. And there's no sense worrying over what will come yet, because we don't know what that will be. So let's just be okay… together."

"Okay, baby," he replies gently, his voice rumbly as he pulls me tighter into him. "Sleep now."

And I do. I fall into a peaceful sleep knowing everything with Ryan is settled and as it should be. Actually, for the first time in a long time, in spite of the fact that my life is kind of a mess, I feel happy.

Sometime later, in the early hours of the morning, when the first bits of gray peek through the dark night, he rolls me to my back and makes love to me one last time, sliding our bodies together as if they were made for each other.

He holds my hands in his by either side of my head, and his mouth covers mine as we come together, breathing each other in.

He places a tender kiss to my mouth one last time, and then I lose him from my body as he climbs out of the bed. He pulls the covers tight around me before he gathers up his clothes and pulls them on then slips from the room.

I hear the quiet snick of a door, and I know he's gone, but this time, I know for sure he will be back.

Everything is going to be okay.

Or so I thought.

SENIOR SENATOR BROKEN HEARTED AS FAIRCHILD SPOTTED WITH PRESIDENT'S AIDE-DE-CAMP

CHAPTER 18

Gone public

One week later

"Are you ready?" Ryan asks me as he parks his SUV in the same lot I parked my car in when I met Gil here for dinner and was waylaid by Jefferson Chancellor and the media.

"As ready as I'll ever be."

"You're lucky you're so cute or else you'd be a real pain in my ass," he says, smiling at me.

"Well, excuse me," I huff.

"It's all right," he says before leaning across the center console and placing a kiss on my lips. "Apparently, being a pain in the ass turns me on."

"You are so not funny," I droll.

"Really? Because I think I'm hilarious."

"Uh-huh."

"You ready now?" he asks.

"Yeah."

And then he climbs down from the driver seat and places his cover on his head. Then he walks around the hood and opens the passenger door for me. He holds a hand out for me, and I take it without hesitation and let him help me down from the giant SUV he drives.

Ryan keeps my hand in his, and we walk into the restaurant's front door. While normally we would go through the back like usual, this week, we're baby-step dating for the world to watch. It's frustrating, because it feels like we were in these beginning stages months ago, and now we're running as fast as we can to catch up.

Last night, Ryan repeated his words of last week that we're going to get married in the near future. It still surprises the hell out of me when he says it, and he brings it up as often as he can. I think he's hoping I get used to the idea so it will happen sooner rather than later.

There are a handful of photographers standing outside the restaurant. Someone must have tipped them off, and I have a funny feeling that someone was Rick. He does excel at such duplicitous actions, after all. Cameras flash, and they call out our names.

"Jules! Jules!" someone shouts.

"Captain Black! Is it true you're date Ms. Fairchild?"

"I think that's pretty obvious," he answers with a happy smile on his face. His southern drawl is enunciated, so he sounds like a friendly, good-time guy.

Ryan pulls open the front door of the restaurant for me as someone shouts another question. "Are you the man in the video?"

I hold my breath and wonder what he's going to say. I know he said he wasn't the kind of guy to let his woman take the fall for him, but I also explained I'm not the kind of woman to ruin a man's career, unintentionally or otherwise. I was pretty sure we had come to an understanding, but the moment of truth is now upon us. Thankfully, he doesn't keep me waiting long.

"No." His voice is clear and calm. If I didn't know better, I would swear he was telling the truth. He's that damn good.

"Does it bother you that there is a sex tape that's gone viral of your new girlfriend and another man?" a reporter asks.

"Yeah," Ryan answers flawlessly. "It does bother me. Jules did not make that tape, as she's already mentioned in previous statements. So someone made it and released it without her knowledge, and it's a crying shame that someone would sink that low. Jules is an honorable and kind woman, which is why I'm involved with her. She does not deserve to be treated this way. Now, if you'll excuse us. We don't have too much time for lunch today."

And then he removes his cover and steps inside after me.

He is perfection.

The hostess shows us to our table and offers us menus, but Ryan declines them. Instead, he proves that not only has he been into me, but he's also paid attention when he orders my favorite meal for me and then his usual for himself. All while I sit surprised.

"What?" he asks with a smile playing about his mouth that is very handsome when the waitress walks away.

"You know me," I blurt out.

"I pay attention," he says casually. "I like to take care of what's mine, and that comes with proper care and attention."

"Shit," I mumble. "You're a good guy."

"I sure do try," he replies, and then the waitress brings our glasses of iced tea to the table. I take a sip of what I think is mine, and it's so sweet I think all my teeth might fall out.

"Yikes," I mutter, pushing his glass across the table to him as he makes a funny face and pushes my unsweet tea to me.

"I don't know how you can drink that stuff." He laughs. "It's so bitter."

"This from the guy who takes his coffee black," I say with a smile.

"Coffee should put hair on your chest, whiskey should burn it back off again, and tea should be sweet just like your mama," he offers.

"I guess my mama's not very sweet," I admit.

"Since I've met her once or twice when I was working for Jake, I can agree with you there," he says, and I feel my cheeks heat. I hate that he knows my parents and that I come from that family. No wonder he didn't want to want me in the beginning; he knew I was born in a viper's den.

"I'm sorry," I whisper.

"What do you have to be sorry for?" he asks, his brows narrowing together.

"That you know that's who I am." I shrug my shoulders.

"You are not them," he says, his voice low in warning. "You are never going to be them."

"I hope not," I admit. "I try not to be."

"You are not them."

"How can you tell?"

"Because I just know," he says, his voice low. "I would not sink my dick in that, and if I thought you were like that, you would have never had me."

"Okay."

"Okay," he agrees, and I squeeze my legs together at the thought of him sinking his dick into me. One would have to agree that Ryan definitely has a way with words.

"So… Texas?"

"Yeah." He smiles now that we're on even footing again.

"What part?" I ask.

"A little itty-bitty town in East Texas called Tall Pines," he answers.

"No kidding!" I laugh. "I have a friend there."

"I know. She married the ball player, right?"

"Yes. Angie," I answer. "She married Cody Reynolds, and they have a little girl now. Do you know them?"

"I'm about ten years older than Reynolds and his crowd," he says. "But like I said, it's a little town, so everyone knows everyone else. I think one of my younger sisters knew him in school."

"You have sisters?" I ask as our lunch is served.

"Two," he answers. "MacKenzie and Amelia."

"What do they do?" I ask, and he smiles proudly.

"They're both Marines."

"You're kidding."

"No, Mack flies F-35s, and Amelia flies the Osprey."

"What's that?" I ask.

"A big helicopter to move people and things," he answers.

"So you're the only one who's not a pilot?"

"Who said I wasn't a pilot?" He laughs. "Our

granddaddy was a Marine, and when he got out, he flew oil pipeline planes, and the girls and I all used to love to go up with him. We've all been flying since we were kids."

"That's crazy."

"There's not much to do in East Texas, and my mom threatened death if we got into trouble with drugs or booze or pregnancy scares, so flying was a lot safer."

"Do you miss it?"

"I have a little Cessna I can take you up in sometime if you'd like," he offers, and I'm not going to lie, the idea of going up in the sky in a tiny little tin can with propellers kind of scares the crap out of me. That must show on my face, because laughter bursts from him. "I take it that's a no."

"It's not a no, per se," I answer, and he laughs again, but this time it's a handsome chuckle. "It's more of a maybe."

"The kids love it," he says. "One day, I'll take you to Texas, and you can see the pipeline path we used to fly."

"I'd like that," I say quietly.

"You'll like Mom and Dad," he says. "Dad's a bit of a loveable grouch, but then again, most old Marines are, and Mom's a doll."

"I'm sure I will." My heart flutters at the thought.

"You ready to meet the kids tonight?" he asks me.

"I'm terrified," I answer honestly. "Last time they

saw me was not good."

"It was not good, because you were worried about their old man," he says. "They're old enough to understand you care about me, and I care about you a great deal. They like that for me, and they're glad I have it. Their mom has had it with Alan for years, and they've wanted it for me too."

"I love that."

"Lacy will like you, because you dress great," he says. "Cabe will like you, because you're hot."

"Ryan!" I gasp and toss my napkin at him, making him laugh again. "Shame on you!"

"What?" He laughs. "He's a seventeen-year-old boy. He's going to notice."

"He is not."

"He will, and I'll tell you how I know."

"Well, how do you know?" I snark.

"Because I noticed right away too."

"You are not a seventeen-year-old boy," I remind him.

"No, I'm not," he agrees with a mischievous smile on his face. "I'm a forty-seven-year-old man, and we all have the same parts."

"You are terrible." I laugh.

"I am," he says. "But I'm also yours."

"That, you are." It falls from my lips so easily I decide not to question it.

And then the waitress brings our bill. Ryan doesn't even let me look at it. He pays and then escorts me out of the building and back to the offices, where we get back to our day.

And that afternoon, the picture of serious Captain Ryan Black with his head thrown back and laughing at something I said with a happy but saucy smile on my face goes viral.

I have never been more terrified of a date before.

I've never dated a man with children—grown or otherwise—before. Although, to be fair, I really haven't dated many men, so there really wasn't very much opportunity for me to date anyone with children.

Ryan's kids aren't really kids at fifteen and seventeen. But they're not quite adults yet either. It's an interesting situation we find ourselves in.

After lunch, Ryan had driven us back to the White House offices, where he went back to whatever it is he does for the president, which I hear is everything from getting coffee to handling his schedule and advising him on military situations. It's an all-encompassing job.

I went back to my office and back to herding the

cluster of cats—both house and feral—who make up the associated press. They were a wild bunch after my lunch date with Ryan. Wanting to know how long we've been going out, if he's the one, and if there are hearts and flowers in the future for us. What they did not ask about was House Bill 2250. A fact that I find most alarming, since Congressman Grissom has since reintroduced it to the House floor, knowing the president has every intention of vetoing it if it goes for a vote.

After my last press briefing, Cara, Grace, and Carter ambushed me in my office, slamming the door behind them.

"So you're meeting the kids tonight?" Cara asked. "This is a big deal."

"This is huge!" Carter agreed.

"Meh, you'll be fine," Grace downplayed the terror coursing through my body. "They're good kids."

It was then I told them about my post Ryan being shot meltdown in the hospital in front of his ex-wife and children. I told them everything. How his son cottoned on really quickly to the fact that his dad meant something to me and how I should have been there, but they didn't know about me to call me to tell me that he'd been injured. When in reality, Ryan and I were not officially a thing then, and my lying to the hospital staff, claiming to be his girlfriend, was more about getting intel than it was actual fact. And how I was afraid to meet them in a normal setting.

"Yikes," Carter said under his breath and Grace sent her elbow back into his gut with a savage smile on her face. My bestie is actually kind of terrifying.

"It'll be fine," she repeated her previous statement.

"What if they think I'm crazy?" I asked.

"Oh, I'm sure they do," Carter mumbled, and Grace went to elbow him, and he blocked her, but her body, rounded with pregnancy, was throwing off her balance, so when she went down, he moved to catch her and took her elbow to the balls, crying out as he did. It was kind of like watching one of those ESPN slow-motion replays during a boxing match where one fighter takes a right cross and their head swings to the side as spit and sometimes teeth come flying out, and we can see the flesh of their cheeks press in on one side and swing out on the other. Only it wasn't cheek flesh that took the impact, but man parts.

"Ouch," I cringed.

"Children!" Cara snapped. "Stop this nonsense. We have more important things to discuss."

"We do?" we all asked in unison.

"Yes!" she snapped.

"Like what, dear?" Grace asked with an encouraging smile on her face.

"Like what she's going to wear."

"Oh my God," I gasped.

"What?" they all asked in unison.

"What am I going to wear?" I shouted.

"I got this," Cara said in a "bitch, hold my beer" tone of voice.

"Yeah, you do," Grace said.

"Get it, girl," Carter added at the same time as Grace, encouraging Cara to do her thing. She is a professional stylist, after all.

"Your blush-pink button-up blouse with the cuffed sleeves, your light wash skinnies with the distressing up the legs, and your bone-colored Louboutins with the pointed toe," she says. "Normal jewelry, soft make-up, bone-colored suede moto jacket."

"Jesus, she's good," Grace muttered.

"God, I think I just came," Carter said, making us all laugh, but then again, he wasn't wrong.

After they left, I grabbed my purse from my desk drawer and made my way through the halls of the offices, smiling at those who smile at me. It surprised me, even though it shouldn't have, that most of the people who knew me and worked with me in the industry for years, or even those who worked with me at the White House for the last few months, know what kind of person I am and stood by me through the sex tape scandal.

It's still available on the internet with millions of downloads per minute, but who cares? It doesn't change who I am and what I stand for. I didn't make it, and it does not define me. I'm just a woman who was a victim for whatever reason. The public thinks it's a classic revenge porn case, that I dumped the guy in the video, and he got mad and took it to the internet. That story couldn't be further from the truth, but then again, who would believe the story of unknown sources trying to blackmail the President of the United Stated and his inner circle? I wouldn't if someone would have told me it was a possibility a year ago, or even a month ago.

So it is what it is, but the people closest to me stood by me. My family, not so much. Even Gil has been surprisingly absent, but then again, in one of my mother's voicemail tirades, she announced that Gil cannot be associated with trash like me, because it would hurt his political career. That is, unless I decided to marry the president's father and let his people spin my current public crisis.

I had my finger in the air and was getting ready to press the Delete button, when the answering machine was swiped out from underneath my hand and ripped from the wall, cords still dangling. I stood there with my jaw dropped as Ryan hurled the entire thing at the wall, where it smashed into a million pieces. Then he just looked at me and said, "Problem solved." And we never talked about it again.

I drove to my home in the suburbs and parked in the driveway. I waved to the last remaining media crews on the lawn. Ryan and I being in the love bubble is not as exciting as a sex tape, so the crowds are thinning. I let myself in and then began my preparations. Cara was right. The outfit was stylish enough to impress but casual enough for dinner at a pizza place.

I'm just transferring the stuff from my regular bag to my cute bone-colored clutch when the doorbell rings. I pull open the door, and Ryan is standing there looking supremely handsome in jeans and a button-down shirt with the cuffs rolled up.

"Hi," I greet him with a nervous smile on my face.

"Babe," is all he says.

"What?" I ask, unsure of how I fucked up before we even get to the restaurant. I figured even I would make it farther than the first two minutes.

"Did you even look to see who it was?" he asks.

"No, why would I? I knew you were coming," I explain, and he looks like he's praying for deliverance—from what, I do not know.

He lets out a heavy sigh before he steps inside and picks up my jacket from the back of a chair. He holds it out for me, and I turn and slide my arms through the sleeves before fluffing my hair out of the collar.

"Ready?" he asks, and I scoop up my bag and grab my keys.

"Ready," I reply, smiling at him.

I lock my front door, and we head down the walk to the driveway, where his SUV sits. Ryan walks me around to the front passenger door and pulls it open for me before offering me a hand to hold as I climb up.

He shuts the door behind me, and I pull my seatbelt across my chest as he walks around the hood and pulls open the driver door and climbs in before looking at me and shaking his head.

"What?" I ask.

"Babe, those shoes are ridiculous."

"I'll have you know I love these shoes," I tell him. "In fact, I could probably run the New York City Marathon in these shoes."

"Really?" he asks.

"Probably not," I admit with a silly smile. "But I'd give it the old college try."

He throws his head back and laughs, and I smile until I hear a delicate giggle and an almost masculine chuckle coming from the backseat and realize we're not alone. I turn and wave with a surprised look on my face.

"Hi."

"Hi," they both say back with friendly smiles on their faces.

"Kids, this is Jules," Ryan introduces. "Jules, this is Cabe and Lacy."

"Hi," I say awkwardly again.

"For the record," Lacy says. "I love those shoes."

"Me too," Cabe adds. "They're sexy as hell."

Ryan laughs again then backs out of my driveway and takes us to dinner at a fabulous pizza place near the capitol. Apparently, the Black family dine here every other Friday night when they're with their dad for the weekend. It's their thing, and they included me. I've never been included in a family thing like this before, and being welcomed into the fold so instantly hits me hard, in a very good way.

After dinner, they drop me back at my house with smiles and waves from the kids, and then Ryan walks me to the front door. After I unlock it, he places a sweet but claiming kiss on my lips and wishes me good night. He waits until after I shut and lock the door behind me, and then he and the kids go home.

It's official. They have claimed me. And Ryan and I have gone public with our budding romance.

Too bad in the days to come that the very foundation of our lives would be shaken, and everything would change.

CHANCELLOR AND
FAIRCHILD SHIPPERS
HOLD OUT HOPE.

CHAPTER 19

King

Oh. My. God.

That's all that keeps circling around and around in my brain. The images play over and over on replay in my mind. This can't be happening.

This morning when I woke up, I would have sworn the birds were singing and the sun was shining. It was like I was living in a fairy tale book. The pages of drawings are so bright and happy. I was happy. I had dressed for work with care in a pair of winter-white wide-leg slacks and a dove-gray silk blouse. I threaded a silver belt through the loops and slipped my feet into a pair of dove-gray Louboutins. I curled my hair delicately around my shoulders and applied soft makeup to my face before threading my diamond studs into my ears and wrapping my watch around my wrist.

I climbed into my car and drove toward the capitol,

stopping at my favorite coffee drive-thru for a skinny vanilla latte and a sesame bagel with cream cheese. You can take the girl out of New York, but you can't take New York out of the girl. I ate in the car and wiped my mouth with a napkin as I pulled into my usual spot in the White House staff parking lot.

I turned off my car and pulled my lipstick from my purse to touch up my face in the sun visor's mirror. I flipped it back up, tossed my lipstick tube back in my purse, and grabbed my keys from the ignition. I made my way through the security line and then headed down the hallway toward my office. I dropped my purse in the bottom desk drawer and fired up my computer.

And that was the last normal thing I did today, because after that, everything changed.

I spot a large manila envelope in my inbox tray, and I scoop it up. My name is printed on the front in bold handwriting, and I wonder what it could be. I don't usually get big packages like this, so it surprises me.

I fold open the little silver prongs and peel back the flap. The envelope is stuffed solid with papers, and I turn it upside down over my desk and shake the contents out.

A stack of glossy black-and-white eight-by-tens and a note scrawled in a masculine hand fall out all over my desk. I pick up the note, and when I read it, my blood runs cold in my veins.

Dear Eagle,

You were warned. Make sure you let Black and Ghost know they were too and that they had this coming. See you at your funeral.

XO

I drop the paper the threat is scrawled on as if it's a coiled-up rattlesnake preparing to strike. And then, as if my hands have a mind of their own, I reach down and pick up the stack of photos. They're of Ryan and me at lunch laughing, of me in a silk robe getting ready for our pizza date, of us with his kids at dinner, of him making love to me in my bed, and of me alone and asleep in my home.

Someone is watching me.

I look around the room and over my shoulder. It's a weird feeling to know someone is watching you without your knowledge. It's a violation. I feel sick to my stomach, and I drop to my knees and lose my bagel and coffee into the wastepaper basket.

I wipe my mouth with the back of my hand and scramble back to my feet. I'm unsteady as the room spins. I grab my phone off the desk and call a number of the only person who I know can help.

"Hello?" Rick answers.

"Rick," I say quickly, and I can hear the tremor in

my voice. I know he does too.

"Honey, what's wrong?" he asks immediately.

"I need to show you something in my office."

"I'll get Black," he says. "He's in a meeting right now."

"No!" I shout. "Don't do that until I'm sure how to approach it."

"It's that bad?" he prompts, his voice low so others can't hear him.

"It's worse."

"I'll be there in five," he says. "Lock the door until I get there."

I hurry to stand and have to steady myself with a hand to my desktop, and then I race over to the door and flip the lock. I press my back to the cool wood and try to still my racing heart and my tumbling stomach. I still feel sick. My forehead is clammy, and I feel hot all over.

There's a knock at the door.

"Jules, it's me," Rick says from the other side of the door, and I flip the lock and let him in.

He shuts the door behind him, and I'm racing back to my trashcan. I throw up again. Poor Rick. This is not what he bargained for.

"Jesus," he says. "Are you okay?"

"No," I gasp and point over to my work area. "On the desk."

I let myself fall down from my knees to my backside as he walks over to my desk. He flips through the photos and reads the note. His face becomes hard, and even I would find him a little terrifying if it weren't on my behalf.

"Fuck," he bites out. "I was hoping you were pregnant."

"You think I'm pregnant?" I squeak.

"You just hurled in a trashcan," he reminds me. "And you and Black are *together* together."

"Yeah, and…?" I ask.

"Two plus two is four, honey," he says gently. He must recognize the confused look on my face. "Are you guys using any protection at all?"

My cheeks burn with embarrassment as I catch his drift. "Umm… no. Not really." His eyes gentle, and I know what he's thinking I'm a Grade-A idiot, because I should have been using some kind of contraceptive instead of enjoying myself and throwing caution to the wind. "I'm probably not pregnant. It's just stress."

"Sure," he says before pulling his cell phone out of his pocket.

"You're not going to tell Ryan I'm pregnant, are you?" I rush to ask, and he smiles at me.

"No, Jules," he tells me gently. "That's for you two to figure out together."

"Thanks," I whisper.

"No problem." And then he begins to unlock his

phone and press a bunch of buttons.

"You said you wouldn't call!" I practically shout, and his eyes cut to me.

Someone on the other end of the line must have answered, because Rick looks back to the photos spread across my desk now and says, "Lock Black down. And get Ghost too. Yeah. It's bad."

And then he ends the call.

"I'm not thinking that was a good conversation," I mutter.

"No, honey, it was not," he says as he delicately stacks the items from the envelope and stuffs them back inside.

He offers me a hand and does not flinch at all that I probably smell like puke. He wraps an arm around my shoulders in a brotherly hug. "It's going to be okay. We won't let anything happen to you."

"It's not me I'm worried about."

"We'll work it out," he says softly.

And then he leads me out of my office and down the hall. He has the envelope tucked under his arm so it's not easily spotted. We make our way through the halls and down to a conference room that is not monitored by closed circuit video cameras.

Rick does not knock; he just pushes open the door where Ryan and Jake are squared off against one another. Gus, Jake's number one Secret Service Agent, steps aside so we can enter, and we do so quietly.

"What the fuck is going on here?" Ryan roars. He's pissed. When Rick said to lock him down, he apparently meant literally. And Ryan does not look happy about it.

"I think I can answer that," Rick says as we push farther into the room.

"Jules?" He takes one look at me and asks, "Are you all right, baby? You look like you've seen a ghost."

There's that word again—ghost. I hope to never hear it ever again.

"No, Ryan," I say with a shaky voice. "I'm not okay."

"What's going on?" he asks again.

Rick produces the envelope from under his arm and holds it up for everyone to see before he begins his explanation.

"This was waiting for Jules in her office inbox this morning when she arrived," he says before opening the little tabs and upending the contents all over the conference table, much like I did this morning.

"What the fuck?" Jake asks with a hard face. Ryan doesn't say anything at all. Instead, he grabs a chair from the table, picks it up, and hurls it into the wall. I let out a little scream and cover my mouth with my hands.

"Come here," Ryan says, and I know he's talking to me, because he's pointing his finger at the ground directly beside himself. When I hesitate, he growls, "I'm not going to ask you again, Jules."

And then I go. I don't waver now. I run directly to him. And when I get close, he holds his arms open, and I hit him full body. He rocks back on a heel to take my weight and then closes his arms around me. I bury my face in his chest and cry.

"No one is going to touch you," he assures, still growling. "Not one fucking hair on your head. Do you hear me?"

I just nod.

"What are we going to do about this?" he asks the men in the room. I clearly have no idea. I knew he was going to lose his mind, so I called Rick. And it turns out I was correct, because when Ryan saw the pictures, he threw a chair. It was impressive when it was my answering machine, but now we're escalating in size and value of the items thrown. At this rate, we'll never be able to keep up financially, and I'm quite rich.

"Honey, what are you thinking?" Jake asks.

"That if Ryan keeps throwing things, I'm going to end up in the poor house trying to replace them," I admit without thinking. "And I'm pretty loaded, so that's saying something."

"Babe," Ryan says, and I tip my head back to look him in the eye. His lips twitch like he's trying not to smile.

"What?" I ask. "It's true. All of it."

I look around, and Gus, Rick, and Jake are all smiling flat out.

"Now that we've gotten that out of the way," Rick inserts, "let's sit down and discuss this. I think we need a plan."

We all sit down around the table, and everyone passes the pictures, and I hand them along, not wanting to look at them for a multitude of reasons, one of them being I don't want to toss my cookies in front of all these people and answer awkward questions. My mind flits back to what Rick said in my office. Could I be pregnant? I just don't know. I make a mental note to find a moment to get to a drug store and buy a pregnancy test.

"She needs full coverage," Ryan says. Well, so much for finding a private time until all this is over.

"We can't justify her having Secret Service coverage," Jake replies. "We would get raked over the coals for it."

"And we can't explain to the public why she needs it," Rick adds.

"I have a buddy," Ryan reminds. "His name's King. He owns King Security. We were in the Marines together until he needed to get out for personal reasons."

"Call him," Jake says.

Ryan produces his phone from his pocket and swipes his finger across the screen to unlock it. He presses a bunch of numbers, and it starts ringing through the room.

"King," a gruff voice answers.

"Hey, man, it's Black," Ryan says.

"Hey, I got some things going down," he says. "Can I call you back in a few days?"

"Actually, I have some things going down too," Ryan replies. "I was hoping you could come and help me keep my girl safe."

"I'm on a… difficult job right now," he tells him. "I can send a man though."

"Can your man take over for you and you head to D.C.?" Ryan asks.

"I fucking wish," King grumbles. "But no. The client wants only me."

"I understand," he says. "I'll let you know what we decide."

"Sounds good, brother. I'll get in touch if this job uncomplicates itself anytime soon."

"All right. Later," Ryan replies before he disconnects. "Fuck."

"It'll be okay," I murmur quietly.

"No, it will not," he bites out. "I'm not playing games with your safety."

"It's not me that I'm worried about," I tell him gently.

"I can't protect you, and I need to make sure you're safe."

"I know," I reply. "So let's keep safe together. Safety in numbers, right?"

"I can't always be with you."

"I know, and I promise to be good. I'll lock myself up in my house when you're not with me. I won't go anywhere alone either."

"If I find out you're taking unnecessary risks...." He trails off, and I wrap my arms around his shoulders.

"I know," I assure. "I won't."

"You better not."

AIDE-DE-CAMP SPOTTED WITH MYSTERY BLONDE AND TONGUES WAG

CHAPTER 20

Promises broken

Three days later

Quiet.

It's been a quiet three days since the threat was delivered to my office. I'm actually wondering if it was a joke or a scam. Not that I would mention either of those ideas to Ryan, who is, to say the least, *unhappy*.

Ryan has to work late tonight, and I promised to go straight home after work. But I have other plans. It's the first time Ryan is letting me out of his sight in three days, and I'm feeling a little stir crazy.

Not to mention that every morning, I toss my cookies like it's my job. And then I'm just fine. When Ryan asks me what's going on, I just chalk it up to stress. But the longer it continues, I think he thinks something else is going on. And honestly, I do too.

I haven't said the words aloud yet, but I think I'm pregnant. Not only am I sick every morning, but I've been crying like… all the time. It's so stupid. I hate crying and almost never do. Now, I'm crying at the drop of a hat.

So enough is enough. After work, I'm heading to a CVS so I can grab a handful of pregnancy tests and figure out what to do next. What I do know for sure is that whatever happens, Ryan and I will do it together.

Since the night I promised him me, we've been together, in every sense, even though we had to keep things under wraps for a little bit longer. Ryan and I are solid, and there is nothing anyone can say to me to make me think otherwise.

I grab my purse from the bottom drawer of my desk and sling it over my shoulder. I make my way through the offices and back through the staff lot to my car. I climb in and head toward my neighborhood.

I pull into the CVS parking lot and get out of my car. The automatic doors open, and the lady working the front counter doesn't even look up as she says, "Welcome to CVS. Happy shopping."

I don't say anything. I just hurry back to the diapers and condoms aisle, where ironically the pregnancy tests are. Whoever plans the aisles for this store has a cruel sense of humor. It's like the three stages of family planning. One, condoms. Two, pregnancy tests, because you forgot the condoms—that one is me. And three, diapers, because you forgot the condoms, and the pregnancy tests told you that you're fucked.

Although, I'm not so sure I'd feel like my life is fucked if I'm pregnant with Ryan's baby. Even as the world feels like it's ending and death threats are hanging over our heads, I know in my heart of hearts I would be over the moon to have a baby with him.

If I'm being honest, I'm in love with Ryan Black. I'm in love with him and his two beautiful children, and I want nothing more than to marry him and be their stepmom and add to that family. All something I never thought I wanted, because I was so busy building my career and living my dreams while my parents were pushing me toward marriage, so I dug my heels in and refused to hear them out every time. I guess it just wasn't the right man, because my life with Ryan is all kinds of right.

I roll my eyes at my hearts-and-flowers thoughts. What kind of sap is he turning me into? Who knew love would make me so soft?

I look back to the pregnancy test choices and realize I should have asked Grace or Cara, or I should have googled something, *anything*, because I have absolutely no idea which one to choose. I wonder if I should call one of my girlfriends. But then I quickly discard that thought, because then I would have to explain, and that would not be good. And besides, I'm in a goddamn CVS. This is not the place to be having life-altering conversations.

But still, I don't know what any of the words say

on the back of the box. Some say **early testing options and** others say **more accurate results.** Are those two options mutually exclusive? I just don't know. So, I grab one of every box on the shelves and pile them into a little basket to carry them up to the front counter.

The cashier stares at my haul wide-eyed, and I stare right back. She must see my terror staring back at her, because she chooses to keep her mouth closed and just scans the eight different pregnancy test boxes.

"Is that all for you tonight?" she asks, and I panic. Is she judging me? I have no idea, but I don't want her to judge me, so I grab a candy bar from the shelf below the counter and hand it to her.

"And this," I say and then grab a cherry-flavored lip balm that looks fantastic too. "And this."

She rings up my extra items and loads them into the plastic shopping bags with my little boxes.

"That will be one hundred and twenty-seven dollars and eighty-six cents," she says, and I feel like my eyes bug out of my head.

Yeesh those little suckers are expensive. My impulse buys at the end couldn't have been more than $2.50 combined. I just quietly pull my wallet from my purse and slide my credit card through the card reader.

"Thank you," I say quietly when she hands me my bags and receipt.

I climb back in my car and feel like I'm going to be sick again, but this time, I know it's just nerves. I drive past a little Japanese restaurant I love. A little teriyaki bento box and some vegetable tempura will hit the spot. What would really hit the spot is some damn sushi, but I know from talking to Grace and Cara during Grace's pregnancy that it's a pretty big no-no, which is a damn bummer, because so is wine. And until I have a yes or a no, both are off the table, because I would not do anything to risk our baby.

I pull my car into the parking lot and park. I grab my purse and toss it over my shoulder as I make my way up to the front of the building. I know I promised Ryan I wouldn't go anywhere but home, and now I've made two stops, but what he doesn't know won't hurt him. Especially if I can give him good news when he hits my place later tonight.

The place is lit up brightly, and it illuminates the windows and the people inside. I'm halfway up the sidewalk in front of the restaurant when I stop in my tracks, and my breath seizes in my lungs.

No.

It can't be. But then again, it is. It looks like mine weren't the only promises broken tonight, because sitting at a booth right near the entrance to the restaurant is a beautiful blonde woman. She's gorgeous. Her hair is bright and shining like she's in a goddamn L'Oreal commercial. She has a wide smile, and you can tell, even from here, that her eyes twinkle when she smiles.

And she's young. Not too young, but much younger than her companion. She's probably five or six years younger than me, putting her right at about thirty years old, and by the look of it, the years have done nothing but enhance her beauty.

But it's not the woman at the table who makes me realize that when I thought fate had finally smiled on me, that my lucky stars had finally found me, I should have known it was all a lie. Because the man she's smiling so brightly at is none other than Ryan Black.

And then my heart smashes into a million pieces in a way that I know it will never be able to be put back together again.

Someone jostles me from behind. "Oh, excuse me," they say. "I'm sorry."

"No," I say quietly. "I am."

Because I'm the one who's really sorry.

They walk past me and into the restaurant. I'm not hungry anymore in a way I'm not sure I'll ever be hungry again. I turn on my heels, get back in my car, and drive myself home.

For the first time in ages, the street in front of my house is empty instead of a news van here or there. Finally, a break in my shitty luck, because what I need is to take these stupid tests into the house and take them.

I pull my car into my garage, grab my purse and my bags, and head into the house, closing the overhead door and locking it behind me. I set my stuff on the kitchen island countertop and pull a glass down from the cupboard. I fill it with water from the sink and drink it down. I fill it up and do it again while staring out at my backyard.

I laugh at nothing in a way that's not funny while I sip my water. Growing up, my parents hated it when I would do things like drink water from the tap. They said it was common, and we weren't common people. Although, judging by the last email I received from my mother, she's changed her mind about whether or not I'm common. She referred to my romance with Ryan as common and said I was just a common whore. I'm trash and nothing but a disappointment. If only she could see me now.

I set my glass in the sink. I'll deal with it later. I continue to look out the back window, and then it dawns on me. I know how he's getting in the house. My hide-a-key rock is sitting right off the porch. And it glows a bright blue. How dumb could I be?

I hurry to the sliding glass door and fling it open. I rush out and grab the entire fake rock and rush back inside with it in my arms. I toss it under the kitchen sink, where he will never find it, and then I make sure every door and window is locked tight.

After I'm done with that chore, I am just done—period, end of. I grab my CVS bags off the counter, carry them upstairs to my bedroom, and drop them all on the bed. I change out of my work clothes and put on my frumpy sweats. I toss my hair up on top of my head and secure it with a rubber band, and then I grab the bags of pregnancy tests and carry them into the bathroom.

I upend the bags on the big marble counter and tear the top off a box. I pull out the instructions. It all looks easy enough. Open the test, pee on the stick, and then wait three minutes. So I take each and every test, and then I line them up in neat little rows like soldiers on my bathroom counter.

Cara always says "a watched pot never boils," so I leave the room. I pop open the new pot of lip balm and swipe some on, and then I rip into my candy bar and decide to drown my feelings in chocolate and peanuts.

I lie back on the pillows on my bed and just begin to settle in when I hear a knock on the glass door in the kitchen, which is directly downstairs from my bedroom. The open stairwell goes a long way to hearing the noises, which makes all of Ryan's past breaking-and-enterings more miracle and magic than they already were.

I know who it is. There's no one else who would be down there at this hour, let alone in the backyard. I want to ignore him, but I shouldn't. I need to just get this over with like a grown up. So I make my way down the stairs and see Ryan looking like his face is made of thunder. I have no idea what he could be pissed at me about.

I unlock the door and slide it open a tiny bit, barring his entrance from my home. If I thought he was mad before, he's certifiably pissed now.

"What the fuck?" he asks.

"I think it's best if you go," I say quietly. "And don't come back."

"Can I ask why?"

I wait a beat and swallow back the tears I haven't

yet cried over him before I answer. "I saw you tonight. I know you lied when you said you were working late. And I also know you were with a woman."

"And?"

"And you don't deny it?"

"I was supposed to work late, but MacKenzie called and asked me to dinner," he says. Hearing her name spoken allowed is like a knife to my belly, and my heart feels like it breaks all over again. His face softens when he sees my crestfallen expression.

"I think you should go," I say again. I'm going to cry. I stayed so strong for the last hour, and now it's all going to come out. I think he's going to leave, but then he puts his palm to my belly and gently shoves me back a step so he can follow me through the door. Once he's inside, he shuts the door behind himself and throws the lock too. "I asked you to go."

"We'll get to that in a minute," he says. "But first, let's talk about the other bullshit you spewed a minute ago."

"What bullshit?" I question. Everything I told him was true.

"Let's talk about the woman you saw me with to-night," he says.

"I'd rather not."

"I'm sure you'll change your mind when I tell you who she is," he states with a smile on his face.

"Too young for you, that's who she is," I mutter

under my breath.

"That—" He laughs. "—and she's also my kid sister, so that's all kind of eww."

"What?"

"That was MacKenzie, my baby sister."

"The one who flies jets?" I ask stupidly.

"That's the one." He smiles gently at me. "She's in town for training before she deploys again. So she looked up her old brother and asked him to dinner. I tried to see if you wanted to come with and meet her, but you had already left the building and weren't answering your cell phone."

"Oops."

"Yeah, oops."

"I'm sorry," I say instantly.

"That's all right, baby," Ryan replies gently. "But what's not all right is assuming the worst of me and then locking me out without giving me a chance to talk it through with you."

Shit. He's right. I did do that.

"I'm sorry," I say again.

"Good. Now kiss me."

And I do.

I press up on my tip toes, and Ryan lets me kiss him for about two seconds before he takes over the kiss. I open my mouth under his when he licks my bottom lip and moan into his mouth.

When he breaks our kiss and I drop back to my heels, he leans forward and puts a shoulder to my belly and lifts me up, making me let out an "eep!" He carries my like a sack of potatoes up the stairs and drops me unceremoniously onto the bed, where I bounce but only once, because he follows me down and covers my body with his.

And there's something about all the emotions that are riding me hard and the way he wants me that sets me on fire, and I go wild. I pull at his clothes, and he pulls at mine, and when we're finally naked and pressed together on the bed, Ryan parts my legs and slides deep inside me.

"Yes," I breathe. He feels so big inside me with no preamble, and I want more than anything for him to move.

I wrap my arms around his shoulders, and he grabs my thigh in his hand and wraps my leg around his waist. And then he finally moves. He holds me tight as he draws back and slams into me, making the bed jerk against the wall.

And then he pulls back and drives into me again and again.

"God, yes."

I rake my nails down his shoulders as he drives into me and wrap my other leg around him and use the leverage to try to draw him deeper inside me. Something about the way I hold onto him, the way I want him, makes him finally snap, and he pounds into me harder and faster with a savageness to him. And it's that beautiful brutality I need to send me over the edge.

Ryan feels me clench around him in my climax, and he calls out my name as he plants himself deep inside me and comes.

We lay entwined in each other for I don't know how long as our breaths intermingle, sawing in and out of our lungs. And then finally he pulls his head from where it was pressed against the crook of my neck and looks me in the eye, and what I see there changes everything. Ryan lets all his emotions he keeps so close to the vest play out across his face—hurt, vulnerability, and last… love.

"Don't try to leave me again," he says quietly.

"I won't."

"Promise me," he orders softly.

"I promise," I say instantly, and he relaxes against me.

"I don't know what I would do if I lost you," he says.

"You won't lose me."

"You have to know, Jules," he says tenderly. "I'm in love with you."

"That's nice," I say gently. "Because I realized recently that I'm in love with you."

It's then that he smiles full-out. In fact, he's still smiling when he presses his mouth to mine. He pulls out and heads to the bathroom to clean up before coming to bed. Something he does regularly. But when he steps in the doorway and flips on the light, I watch as he freezes in his tracks. And it's in that moment I remember all the pregnancy tests.

"Jules?" Ryan calls out.

"Yes, Ryan?"

"You wanna tell me why there's about seven hundred positive pregnancy tests on the counter in here?" he prompts.

"They're positive?" I ask.

"Every last one of them."

"Oh my God," I whisper, and suddenly he's there, crawling on the bed and back over me. He frames my face with his hands and gets close.

"Are you having my baby?" His voice is low and rough, brimming with emotion.

"Yeah."

And then he presses his mouth to mine. I wrap my arms back around him, and Ryan shows me just how happy he is. In fact, he does it rather enthusiastically. And then we fall asleep with smiles on our faces, in each other's arms, never knowing tomorrow would bring nothing but nightmares.

COULD ROCKY
LOVE TRIANGLE
CAUSE RIFT
BETWEEN
POPULAR BFFS
POTUS AND
FAIRCHILD?

CHAPTER 21

Today, I'm going to have a quiet day. I downloaded *What to Expect When You're Expecting* onto my e-reader, and I'm going to veg out and relax while Ryan goes to spend the afternoon with his kids. We've decided not to tell them about the baby yet, because we've only just found out about it ourselves, and I haven't had a moment to get into see an OBGYN.

I'm actually at the point where I may have to ask Grace to pull some favors for me with hers. But that would also mean telling Grace she's not the only one knocked up in this neck of the woods. I kind of just want to keep it to ourselves for a little bit longer.

Ryan kisses me goodbye and then heads out to meet up with the kids for lunch. He's been gone for about an hour when my phone rings.

"Hello?" I answer.

"Hey, sis," Gil says. "I'm in town again. Want to catch lunch with your big brother?"

"I would love that!" I tell him. And I would. I breathe a sigh of relief that we can move on from here. I love my brother and I don't like fighting with him. It's rare that we disagree. Mostly, we're just vastly different people with a huge age gap between us. There was never anything like toys or treats to tangle over because he was mostly grown by the time I came along. I don't like that he's taken our mother's side, but I also know that I can just avoid the conflict until it goes away. Eventually, the media will give up and they will have to as well. I just have to smile and nod my head and then wait them out.

"I'll pick you up in thirty minutes."

"Sounds good," I reply. "I'll be ready when you get here."

"See you then," he says and disconnects.

I jump up and race upstairs. I brush out my hair and twist it into a messy ballet bun and then swipe on some soft makeup, because it would not please my mother to see photos of us and I look like hot garbage. I pull on dark skinny jeans, a blush-pink draped chiffon tank, and a winter-white blazer. I put on my signature jewelry and step into my bone-colored Louboutins.

I'm just walking back down the stairs when there is a knock at the front door. I pull open the door, and Gil is standing on my front porch.

"Ready to go?" he asks me with an easy smile on

his face.

"Absolutely," I reply and lean in to give him a hug.

"Great," he says. "There's this new place I'm dying to try."

"I'm sure it'll be good," I tell him as I lock my front door and head down the walk. I climb in the front seat of his car and buckle my seatbelt. And all the while, I just feel like something is… off.

I brush it off as our having not cleared the air yet since our last dinner. He drives farther and farther away from the city and into a part of town I've never been before. In fact, it doesn't look so great.

"Where are we going?" I ask.

"It's just a little bit farther," he tells me, but he keeps his eyes pinned on the road and doesn't look at me. "We're almost there."

"But where is there?" I ask as he pulls up to an old warehouse. Maybe it's some kind of new popup restaurant. I hear those are all the rage lately.

"Change of plans," Gil says as he reaches for something in the pocket of his door.

"What's that?" I ask, but then he's moving faster than I've ever seen him move before, and I yelp as the needle pierces my neck.

"You should have done what you were told," he snarls, and his face changes to a look of rage that I've never seen on him.

The last words I say to my brother before everything goes black are, "I trusted you."

Never will I make that mistake again.

Probably because I'll be dead.

FUNERAL PLANS ARE PENDING

CHAPTER 22

Mistakes

Ryan

"Everything all right, Dad?" my son asks, and I have the sinking feeling that everything is not all right.

"I don't know," I hedge, not wanting to upset my kids. I tried to call Jules to see if she wanted me to bring her a sandwich home from this little deli I know she likes. But no matter how many times I try to call her, she doesn't answer.

I hang up and try another number. Rick answers immediately.

"Hey, man, what's up?" he asks.

"Not much," I tell him. "Hey, are you guys at home?"

"Yeah, what's going on?"

"I'm not sure. I've been trying to call Jules, but she's not answering."

"I'll head over now," Rick says.

"Thanks, man." And then I disconnect.

"Maybe we should go check on her," my daughter, such a sweetheart, suggests.

"Why don't you guys head back to your mom's," I tell them. "And I'll go check on Jules."

"I hope she's okay," Lacy says.

"I'm sure she's fine," I lie. By the look on my son's face, he knows something's wrong. I just don't know what yet.

I hug my kids goodbye, climb in my SUV, and head back to Jules's house, all the while knowing it was a mistake to have left her alone today.

RICK

"What was that?" Cara asks me.

"That was Ryan," I answer immediately. "He said Jules isn't answering the phone, and he's worried about her."

"I hope everything's okay," my beautiful wife says.

"I'm sure it is," I lie, not wanting to upset her if something is not right with one of her closest friends. I won't be able to shield her from it, but I can do my best to soften the blow if I can. "Do me a favor and call Jake and give him a heads up."

"Of course," she says.

I slide my feet into a pair of running shoes and grab my keys off the hook. I kiss my daughter's forehead where she sits putting together a puzzle on the coffee table in front of her mother. And then I drop a kiss on Cara's lips and touch my palm to her slightly rounded belly. We're not telling anyone yet, but I'm over the fucking moon.

And then I walk out the door, climb in my SUV, and head toward Jules's house, knowing the entire time we've made too many fucking mistakes with this mess. I should have pushed and demanded more answers. I shouldn't have let Jake convince me to go in soft. When someone is blackmailing the President of the United fucking States, you demand action and retribution.

And I did not. I went in soft and have nothing to show for it.

I pull up in front of her house, and I instantly know something is wrong. As in really fucking wrong. It's too still. And the hair on the back of my neck stands on end. I don't like it.

When Ryan pulls up behind me and lets us into the house, I know just how wrong it all is.

We've made way too many fucking mistakes. And now Jules and Ryan are going to pay the ultimate price.

Fuck.

JAKE

My phone rings.

"Hello?" I answer.

"Hey, Jake, it's Cara," she replies. "Something's up with Jules, and Ryan can't get ahold of her. Rick is going over there to check things out, and I think Ryan is going to meet him there. I'm sure it's overkill, but Rick told me to call you and tell you what's going on."

"Thanks, honey," I tell her. "I'll look into it."

"Thanks."

"All right, I'll call you in a bit when I know more."

"Thanks, Jake," she says. "Hug Grace for me."

"I will," I reply and then disconnect.

Fuck. This is not good.

"What's going on?" Grace asks. Shit. She moves like one of those damn cats she loves so much. I don't even hear her coming anymore, and they call *me* Ghost. I'm clearly getting soft in my old age.

"Not much," I lie. "I'm just going to step into the hall and make a phone call."

"Okay," she says. "Hurry back."

"I will."

I don't step into the hall, but I do leave the room. I go to a hidden safe I have stowed away in the back of the closet, punch in the code, and pull out an unregistered Colt 45. I tuck it into the back waistband of my jeans and then step out into the hall.

"Sir," Gus greets me. Thank God he's here today. He's one of few people I can trust.

"Ryan can't get ahold of Jules," I tell him immediately. "Rick and Ryan are both on their way to her house now."

"What would you like me to do, sir?" he asks.

"I know you're on duty today and you can't leave your post, and I wouldn't ask you to," I say. "But could you keep a line of communication open with them?"

"Yes, sir," he says, and then he leaves the room.

I'm just about to follow him, when the door opens and my father steps inside.

"What are you doing here?" I ask.

"I need you to be quiet and listen," he tells me.

"There is nothing you have to say that I want to hear."

"It's about Jules and Black," he states, and suddenly I'm listening. He knows he has my attention and smiles. "It's bigger than you realize." My father always was a fan of theatrics and drawing it all out. I can't stand it.

"Get on with it."

"It was never about her," he says. "She was just a pawn. Like you were supposed to be, but you won't play the game."

"What game?" I ask.

"The one where America falls."

"You're a traitor?" I question, and color me surprised. An asshole, sure, but a traitor to his country? I had no idea.

"Traitor is such an ugly word," he says. "I prefer businessmen."

"And how do you figure that?"

"Because they pay better," he replies. "But Jules didn't play her part, and they're going to kill her for it."

"What was her part?" I hope to God I can get the information out of him before it's too late.

"She was supposed to marry you, and when she couldn't seal that deal, she was supposed to marry me."

"And what would that have done?" I ask as the door swings open and a gun goes off. I watch in shock as my father falls to the floor with a hole in his chest and dies.

I look to the door where Mark Jeffries stands with a gun in his hand, staring at where my father had been previously standing.

"He was always weak," Jeffries says.

"That's true," I agree. I mean, what else am I supposed to fucking say here? He's not exactly wrong.

"I knew he would come right here and spill his guts to you, because he was fucking weak," he snarls. "You all are. Why couldn't you just do what you were supposed to?"

"Which was?"

"Marry my daughter! That was her only job. She was bred to do it," he explains.

"According to my father, I thought I was supposed to marry Jules."

"That was never my plan. They wanted that."

"Who is they?" I ask, but he's raising his gun toward me.

"And you couldn't do what you were supposed to, and now you have to die," he says. "You all have to die."

"Who is they?" I repeat on a shout as he pulls the trigger.

The shot goes wide. I dive behind a sofa and pull the gun from my waistband. And then I hear another gunshot go off. I jump up from behind the couch and run to where Jeffries is lying on the floor in a pool of his blood.

Rhys is standing in the doorway, holding a gun in one hand and talking on his phone that's in the other.

"Sorry, hun," he says. "I'm going to have to let you go now."

"Who is they?" I ask Jeffries as I drop to my knees beside him.

"Fairchild," he whispers, and then he dies.

"I got here as soon as I could," Rhys tells me.

"Are you going to get into trouble for this?" I ask,

and then Gus steps out from the next room with his gun pointed at me.

"There just isn't any good help anymore," Rhys drolls.

"Not you too, Gus."

"No hard feelings, Ghost," he says. "I'm sorry it has to be this way."

And then he raises his gun.

And he's shot in the back by Leo, the Secret Service Agent I never liked.

"Jesus Christ!" Rhys shouts. "This is like that bloody *Clue* movie where *everyone* did it."

"You too, I take it?" I say, preparing to take down a protection agent that I never really liked and it turns out I was right all along.

"No," Leo says, and his voice changes to a deep brogue much like Rhys's. "I'm deep cover."

"For who?" I ask, hating that someone managed to get past my trusted people. Although, then again, Gus was my trusted people and he just tried to kill me. That does pose a problem.

"For me," Rhys answers. "And you thank bloody hell for that one at least."

My thoughts exactly.

RYAN

I know something's wrong the minute I pull up to the house. Rick is standing at the door knocking, but I know in my gut she's not there.

I run up the steps and use my key, the one I took from that stupid rock when I found where she stashed it under the kitchen sink when she tried to break up with me over a stupid misunderstanding with my sister, of all people, and I unlock the front door.

There's a note on the stone tile. The same tile I fucked her on when we didn't know each other but were drawn to each other like magnets. And I left her there like an ass. We could have had so much more time together, and I fucked it up. I've made one mistake after another where Jules is concerned. I can only hope it doesn't cost us in the end.

I pick up the note and read it. I know immediately she didn't leave it. Rick, on the other hand, has a sorry expression on his face.

Ryan,

I'm leaving you. I've gone to stay in an apartment at the old Fisher's King Ware-house. Don't come looking for me.

-J

"It's not what you think," I tell him.

"Are you sure?" he asks. "Because it looks like she left you."

"She's pregnant," I tell him. "We just found out yesterday and made love all night to celebrate."

"Fuck," he says quietly. "I had my suspicions last week."

That's news to me. I had wondered who she talked to about it. Actually, I didn't think she talked to anyone at all, since she wanted to keep it quiet. I figured it was just something that girls know. Like hey, you're pregnant.

"Besides," I tell him. "This is her house. I still have my own across town. If we were breaking up, she would just stay here."

"Think it's a trap?" he asks me.

"One hundred percent."

"Think she's there now?" he asks.

"I don't know," I say as I pull my phone out of my pocket. "But I'm going to find out."

I call up the Find My Phone app and bring up her phone. When I was worried about her security and she told me she wouldn't go anywhere without me, I knew that was bullshit, even if she thought she was telling the truth. Jules can be a little reckless at times, and I figured this was no different. And I turned out to be right last night when I realized she went to the drugstore and almost to dinner, when she told me she would go straight home. So I made her trackable by her phone. And thank God I did.

"Yep," I say, watching the little circle ping near the warehouse. "Looks like that's where her phone is at least."

"Let's go," Rick says to me. I jump in the passenger seat of his SUV, and we head out.

SECRET PLOT TO TAKE DOWN THE PRESIDENT'S INNER CIRCLE

CHAPTER 23

Stupid girl

Jules

Lights.

Lights are bright, and my head is pounding. My head is pounding, and my mouth feels like it's full of cotton, and my throat is dry.

I blink my eyes against the bright lights, and it all comes back to me. Gil, my brother, the only person to ever treat me right in the house of horrors we grew up in, turned on me.

I look around. I'm sitting in a chair, my body taped to it, and I'm in a warehouse. We were supposed to be going to lunch, but we stopped here instead. I can't believe I thought it was one of those popup things. I'm so stupid.

Actually, I can't believe I trusted Gil. That was

even worse.

"Look who's finally joined our party," my mother purrs. This just keeps getting better and better.

I turn my head to look at her, and stars explode across my vision. Someone punched me in the face.

"What was that for?" I ask.

"For not doing what I told you to, you stupid, stupid girl," she snarls before Gil hits me again. I feel my lip tear open, and I taste blood.

"Please stop," I whisper. "I'm pregnant."

I don't know why I thought the knowledge of their impending grandchild and niece would make them let me go. I guess I'm as stupid as she thinks I am. Because Gil hits me again. I had no idea he could pack such a punch. I thought he played golf and squash. I didn't know he could beat the shit out of someone. Or that that someone would be me, but I digress.

"Why are you doing this?" I gasp.

"Why else?" She laughs. "Power and money."

"I can get you power," I tell them. "I work for the president." Maybe if I bargain, they'll let me go. Wishful thinking, I know.

"He doesn't have the kind of power I want," she says.

"And what kind is that?" I ask. I shouldn't; I know I shouldn't have asked as soon as the words are out of my mouth, but my brain hasn't caught up with whatever they gave me in the car.

"Global power," Mom replies.

"I thought Gil wanted to be president?" I ask.

"He does," she replies. "Just not of this country."

"What?"

"When America falls, who will replace it?" Gil prompts. When I don't respond, he answers for me. "I'll be with the nation that's waiting in the wings to replace us."

"You're a traitor?" I gasp.

"That's such an ugly word," my brother laughs.

"If you'd have just married Jefferson like you were supposed to, this wouldn't be happening, but just as always, you almost ruined everything," Mom snaps. "Do you know how much we got paid to offer you up to them? And we had to pay it all back, you selfish bitch."

Sold. My parents fucking sold me so my crazy brother could rule the world. This is insane. Stuff like this just doesn't happen in real life.

"Now he's dead, and soon, so will you be too," Gil says with a nasty smile.

"Jefferson died?" Mother asks. "What a pity. I liked him."

"He was weak," Gil says.

"That's true too."

"Mark killed him," Gil says conversationally, and I know he's playing with me before I die. "But then Gus killed him. Did you know Gus? But then, of course you did. Tell me, who did you think took the video of you whoring yourself to the captain?"

"No."

"That's right. Gus is a true patriot," he says with a mean smile. "And just about now, he's dispatching your president and his wife."

"No!"

"I think we need to rough her up a bit more," my mom says. "It needs to look like Black beat her to death."

"No!" I scream once more, and then the room explodes.

Ryan and Rick burst into the room. Gil tries to fight them, but my asshole brother is no match for two of the strongest military men I've ever met in my life, and Ryan takes him down quickly. I think it's finally over, but then my mother produces a small gun from her pocket.

I scream, and Ryan turns around just in time to be shot in the chest. He drops to his knees, his face going white. *No, no, no, no, no.* This can't be happening.

"Change of plans," she says as she turns the gun on me. "You are not going to ruin my plans for your brother and me."

"I won't," I say. "I promise."

"You can't not," she sneers. "You ruin everything. Ever since the day you were born, you've been ruining things."

I see Leo, the Secret Service Agent no one likes because he's such an asshole, step into the room. He must be dirty, just like Gus. He's going to kill us all. I send up a quiet *I'm sorry* and *I love you* to Ryan and close my eyes.

I flinch when the gun goes off. And I wait to die. And then I wait some more. And then finally, I open my eyes and realize I'm not dead, but my mother is. Leo is cuffing Gil, and his team is dragging him out. Rick is cutting through the tape that binds me to the chair.

"Ryan," I whimper when I look at him.

"He's going to be okay," Rick assures me.

Thank God. He's really got to stop getting shot like this.

Later, at the hospital, I sit with Ryan's family while he's in surgery. It wasn't as bad as it seemed. He wears his grandfather's dog tag on his chain with his own, and his grandfather's had stopped the bullet from killing him. It was no small miracle.

I was also checked out, and everything is fine. Ryan and I are expecting a baby in just eight short months.

Gil was taken off to parts unknown by Leo and his team. Gus, Jefferson, Mark Jeffries, and my parents are all dead. They had been behind HB 2250, the bill Jake staunchly opposed. The one that would give the bulk of the United States's power, money, and weapons to a variety of nations we're not exactly friendly with. If their bill had gone through, the U.S. would have been ripe for the picking, and then someone was waiting in the wings to take our place and the head of the world's table. I don't know why or when, but it was always my brother, Gil. How he could think that he could take down a nation like that, I will never know. All I know is Jake was right when he said it was dangerous.

Jake, Rick, and Ryan are going to be busy cleaning up Washington when he's all healed up; at least, that's what Jake says. I have a funny feeling Rick and Ryan will be up for the task though.

As for me, I haven't decided if I'm going to stick it out as the White House Press Secretary. I guess you could say my priorities have drastically changed. I'm taking a small break to decide what I'm going to do. All I know is I'm going to spend as much time with Ryan and the kids as I possibly can. After that… who knows?

NEW INTERVIEW SHOW TOPS CABLE CHARTS.

Former Press Secretary Hits Ratings Gold

EPILOGUE

Forever

Eight years later

"And that's it for this edition of *True Story with Julia Black*," I say as the camera pans in on me. It's the way I end my interview show every week.

"Thank you so much, Jules," Cody says as he wipes his eyes.

"He is such a baby," Angie says off camera.

"Nah." I laugh. "He did good. Besides, it's the ten-year anniversary of the accident that broke his spine and changed his life."

"But did he have to cry?" she asks.

"Eh." I smile. "They all do."

We step out of the formal living room in the ranch-style house I share with Ryan and our four children: Emily, Abigail, and twins Ricky and Jake, named after their favorite uncles. Lacy and Cabe also have places here, although we don't see them very often. Lacy is off "finding herself," much to Ryan's chagrin, and Cabe is serving out his second enlistment in the Marines. When he graduated bootcamp, Kristen and I cried in each other's arms while her husband Alan looked terrified, and Ryan just shook his head and muttered, "Women." Whatever that means.

After Jake's last term, Ryan and I retired to Tall Pines, Texas, where I host a top news interview show once a week for my old friends at Eagle News Network. A contract I brokered when Ryan and I sold them my story.

Jake, Rick, and Ryan, true to their promise, cleaned up Washington, and it took them quite a bit to do it. After an international incident involving a crowned prince, they decided to hang up their superhero capes and just be normal everyday politicians.

Tonight is Ryan's fifty-fifth birthday, and I have a big surprise for him. One I was even surprised to discover myself, but just like the first time, Rick was the one who cottoned on to the idea first—then again, they have three of their own.

Lucky number seven is on its way. I'm going to give him the good news after his party.

After everything we've been through, I love every blessing that comes our way while we continue to build our forever.

THE END

PLAYLIST

So What—P!nk

Hot Girl Bummer—Blackbear

Truth Hurts—Lizzo

Come Over—Sam Hunt

I May Hate Myself—Lee Ann Womack

Black—Dierks Bentley

I Hope—Gabby Barrett

One Last Time—Ariana Grande

Why The Call It Falling—Lee Ann Womack

Good As Hell—Lizzo

Blinding Lights—The Weeknd

If the World Was Ending—JP Saxe & Julia Micheals

Just Might—Sugarland

Graveyard—Halsey

Meant to Be—Bebe Rexha ft. Florida Georgia Line

ABOUT THE AUTHOR

Jennifer is a thirty-something lover of words, all words: the written, the spoken, the sung (even poorly), the sweet, the funny, and even the four-letter variety. She is a native of San Diego, California where she grew up reading the Brownings and *Rebecca* with her mother and *Clifford and the Dog who Glowed in the Dark* with her dad, much to her mother's dismay.

Jennifer is a graduate of California State University San Marcos, where she studied Criminology and Justice Studies. She is also a member of Alpha Xi Delta.

Thirteen years ago, she was swept off her feet by her very own sailor. Today, they are happily married, and the parents of an eleven-year-old and nine-year-old twins. She lives in East Texas, where she can often be found on the soccer or baseball fields, drawing with her children, reading, or wondering what the hell her favorite senior citizens have gotten up to now. Jennifer is convinced that if she puts her Fitbit on one of the dogs, she might finally make her step goals.

She loves a great romance, an alpha hero, and lots and lots of laughter.

STALK HER
(She loves that shit)

Website
www.jenniferrebeccaauthor.com

Facebook
www.facebook.com/JenniferRebeccaAuthor

Instagram
www.instagram.com/JenniferRebeccaAuthor

Twitter
www.twitter.com/JenniRLreads

Pinterest
www.pinterest.com/JenniferRebeccaAuthor

Bookbub
www.bookbub.com/authors/jennifer-rebecca

Book+Main
www. bookandmainbites.com/JenniferRebecca

And join her reader group on Facebook:
The Dangerous Dames
www. facebook.com/groups/JRdangerousdames

ALSO BY JENNIFER

A Presidential Affair
The Senator's Secret
Caught by the Chief of Staff
The Press Secretary's Passion

Royal Secrets and Lies
King of Lies
Crown of Thorns
Save the Queen

The Claire Goodnite Series
Tell Me a Story
Tuck Me in Tight
Say a Sweet Prayer
Kiss Me Goodnight
By the Light of the Moon
The Complete Claire Goodnite Series

The Liam Goodnite Series
Hush Little Baby
Don't Say a Word

The Funerals and Obituaries Series
I Met a Girl
Dead and Buried
Dead and Gone
Dead and Deceived
Dead and ... Wed?

The Murder on Ice Series
Attack Zone
Layback

The Southern Heartbeats
Stand, Volume 1
Joy
Whiskey Lullaby, Volume 2
Mercy
Just a Dream, Volume 3, Coming 2021

Stand Alone Titles
Trap: A Salvation Society Novel

KING OF LIES

nd So It Goes

Run!

My brain is screaming at me to run. I have to go. I have to get out of here. I'm not safe here anymore. I think I knew it all along that I wasn't safe here but I was living in a dream. A beautiful dream where Prince Charming fell for a shy, mousy girl like me and swept her off her feet and straight into a fairytale.

I should have known that it was all a lie.

Guys like that don't fall for girls like me. I wasn't cut out to be a princess and I never will be. I should have kept my eyes open and not fallen for the fantasy.

Even with a viper in my bed, I should have run then but I didn't. I can only hope now that it isn't too late. He promised me long ago that if I ever wanted to, I was free to go, but that I wouldn't be welcome back. I pray he keeps his end of the promise.

I pack only what I need in a backpack and shove the stack of papers and photographs, the truth to his lies on top. I zip it closed and sling one strap over my shoulder. He can keep the dresses and jewels, I don't have any use for fancy things like that back home.

"Ma'am?" Leo, my personal security officer asks when I open the door.

"I need to get to the airport," I tell him. "Right away."

He looks at me, his blue eyes watch and survey and I know that they see the truth. I'm running and I'm not even going to try and hide it.

"Have you spoken to His Royal Highness about this urgent matter?"

"Not yet," I reply.

"Maybe you should—" he starts.

"The car, Leo," I interrupt him.

"Yes, ma'am," he says. "I'll get it straight away."

"Thank you, Leo… for everything."

"It's been my pleasure ma'am."

And then he heads down the hall to arrange the car. I follow on his heels. There's so much I will miss here, mostly people I have met. And there is also a lot that I won't miss at all. Again, mostly people.

Harris, the driver assigned to me when I leave the castle without Rhys pulls around the corner and jumps out of the driver's seat. He opens the rear door for me and I slide inside. Leo climbs in the front passenger seat with his phone to his ear. He might be tattling on me but I don't care.

Not anymore.

"Where to, Miss?"

"The airport," I answer.

"Are you meeting His Royal Highness?" he asks

me. "And should I return to the castle for the rest of your luggage, ma'am?"

"No," I answer his questions softly. I can hear the catch in my voice and so can Harris and Leo. "I won't be coming back."

Harris drives us through the castle gates and down the long and winding road that leads to the highway or whatever it is they call it here. It's a two lane road that twists and turns down through the hills before it spreads out to four lanes across under a huge bridge.

The piano strains of an old Billy Joel tune fill the car softly, reminding me that life isn't sunshine and rainbows and I need to remember that more hard knocks are handed down than not. And I should have already learned this particular lesson long before Rhys Alexander crashed into my life and made me fall in love with him.

But that's just how it goes.

My phone rings and I press my eyes closed. I know exactly who it is. I don't want to answer but that's not right. I slide my finger across the cool glass to unlock it.

"Hello?" I answer.

"Where are you?" he demands, his brogue deeper and thicker than normal.

"I'm leaving," I say quietly.

"Why?"

"I know," I whisper. "I know it all."

"You don't know the half of it," he says after a beat.

"I know it was all fake," I say. "Every last bit of it."

"Come back," he changes the subject. "I'll meet you at the castle."

"I can't do that." The car lurches to the right but I ignore it.

"I'll come to you," he offers.

"No," I whisper with my heart clenching painfully in my chest. "We had a deal."

The car lurches again.

"Where are you?" Rhys asks and I look out the window and see that we're almost to the big overpass just before the exit for the airport.

"It doesn't matter," I whisper. "I'm already gone."

"No."

"Ma'am," Leo says. "I need you to put your seat-belt on."

"What's happening?" Rhys demands.

I move as fast as I can to comply. I drop my phone down to the bench next to me. I hear Rhys's voice yelling for me but I can't understand what he's saying.

"What's going on?" I ask.

"Don't worry, ma'am," Harris says.

"Watch out!" Leo yells and then the car is filled with the sounds of breaking glass and crunching metal.

My face smashes against the window next to me

and an explosion of pain blasts through my face and in my brain.

I should have known. I should have run when I had the chance. I was never safe here. Not in this country, or in his castle, and I was absolutely never safe with Rhys.

"Stella!" I hear him shout. "Hen! Answer me!"

When the car comes to rest, only the last bits of of the song can be heard through the car and I sing the last line, a fitting end to my tragic tale, a life where if something awful could happen it would and the losses compound one after another. I should have stayed hidden in my quiet life all alone.

I had thought that he was my Prince Charming. That he was whisking me off to a fairytale life in a faraway land. But He's not Prince Charming, Rhys Alexander is the King of Lies.

"And so it goes…"

"Hen!" he screams one last time, or more, I don't know.

And then the blackness overwhelms me and I fade into nothing…

Once upon a time,

A girl was swept away to a castle in a faraway land,

by a handsome prince.

But when she looked around there were no princes,
no kings and queens and no happy endings.

Only monsters.

ACKNOWLEDGEMENTS

THANK YOU SO MUCH for reading Jules and Ryan's story in THE PRESS SECRETARY'S PASSION. I so hope that the end of these stories leaves you feeling like they all got what they needed in the end. I so love when flawed characters find their forever person. Of course with a few twists and turns along the way. Thank you for reading this book.

The rest of these thank yous won't go like they usually do. While writing this book, my dad became very ill. For those of you who have met and fallen in love with my dad at signing events, you know that he's not your typical 72 year old. He's strong and healthy. He works out daily and eats healthy foods, something I don't understand, but I digress. He is healthy and on the mend but it rocked our world to see such a strong man brought so low.

You have a book to read because of the following people: Tricia Crouch, my fantastic PA and life runner. She jumped in and got shit handled the second she found out there was a family emergency. Kayla Robichaux, my editor, who often keeps me on track when I fall off. She makes sense out of the words that come out even when I can't. This time was so much more. I can't even begin to describe how much she sorted me out all while making sure my family was ok. And Emma and Stacy who offered to buy meals from as far as four hours away to across the world. They lovely ladies made sure we were ok and I know they were with us.

And last but not least, Alyssa Garcia, my publicist, graphic designer, bestie boo, rid or die. She kept me on track, she took my kids, and she ran across the street in the middle of the night towards an ambulance. I couldn't have taken care of my people and finished this book without her.

And also my other bestie boo, my long time ride or die, Stephanie and her husband Reo who checked up on mom and I daily to make sure we were ok. To offer to run groceries or whatever else we might need.

And also thank you for those who won't ever see this. Our friends and neighbors who stopped what they were doing, who ran next door, to help out my mom and to advocate for my dad when Sean or I were not there. Who opened doors and then closed them when I freaked out that my dad's cats would get loose. (Remember the ladder incident?) Chrissy, Lee, Alyssa, and Adrian, thank you from the bottom of my heart. I'm so thankful that when we convinced mom and dad to move here with us it was to be surrounded by wonderful people.

Tonight, my son described our friends as the family God chose for us. Not the family we were born into, who we need, but the ones he knew we needed in our lives to make it better. At first I thought, what in the Big Love kinda hell is he talking about? But then it just clicked. He was right. These are the people we need to make our lives better, not just in an emergency or when we get something from it but always. To laugh with, to cry with, to celebrate joys and grieve heavy losses. I'm so glad this time we get to celebrate.

And last but never least, the blue eyed boy who stole my heart. I knew he was a good guy the night I met him, I knew he was a great man when I watched him hold his baby, and I saw his kind and patient heart as we get to grow old together and watch our children grown from babies who need us to independent people. But I also get to see the bond that he shares with my parents, his parents, our friends and family. I'll love him in this life and the next. And I'm forever thankful that his beautiful heart decided on mine.

It was only ever you, babe.